RISE OF THE WITCH
WITCHES OF KEATING HOLLOW
BOOK SEVENTEEN

DEANNA CHASE

Copyright © 2025 by Deanna Chase

Editing: Angie Ramey

Cover image: © Ravven

ISBN 978-1-965804-10-0

All rights reserved. No part of this publication may be reproduced, stored in, or introduced into a retrieval system, or transmitted in any form, or by any means (electronic, mechanical, photocopying, recording, or otherwise) without the prior written permission of both the copyright owner and the publisher of this book.

This book is a work of fiction. Names, characters, places, and incidents are products of the author's imagination or are used fictitiously. Any resemblance to actual events, locals, business establishments, or persons, living or dead, are entirely coincidental.

Bayou Moon Press, LLC

www.deannachase.com

Printed in the United States of America

ABOUT THIS BOOK

Briggs Williams has a problem. For years he'd been unable to control his magic. But all that changed when he moved to Keating Hollow. There's just something about the enchanted town that settles him. But when an old flame shows up in Keating Hollow out of the blue, his magic flares out of control again. Suddenly he's a walking disaster. And there appears to be only one person that can help him keep his magic in check—Melissa Benson, the one woman he wants but knows he can never have.

Melissa Benson is determined to find her Mr. Right, instead of Mr. Right Now. If only she had a little bit of magic, she'd cast a love spell to help her find him. Unfortunately, she's never been magical. It appears her only talent is dating emotionally unavailable men. Which is why she has sworn off the very handsome Briggs Williams, who has made it clear he's not interested in anything permanent. But when his ex walks into town and Briggs asks Melissa to pretend to be his fiancée, she finds herself unable to refuse his insane request. Now she's spending all her time with a man she can't resist who is destined to break her heart.

Just when Melissa is determined to break off the charade, it becomes clear that she has magic after all, and if she leaves Briggs's side now all hell will break loose. In order to keep Briggs and the residents of Keating Hollow safe, Melissa has no choice but to go through with the fake engagement at least until Briggs can regain control of his magic. But will she lose her heart in the process, or will she and Briggs find they can't live without each other after all?

CHAPTER 1

Briggs Williams stared down at the gorgeous brunette next to him and grinned. Melissa, his fake fiancée for all of about thirty seconds, had her hands curled into fists and looked ready to spit nails. He couldn't deny that in that moment she was a major turn on. But it wasn't like he could do anything about it in the middle of the Townsend's brewery. Especially not when his semi-famous ex-fling happened to be standing in front of them, undressing him with her eyes.

"Excuse me," Melissa said as she stared pointedly at Kassie Kinny's fingers that were lingering on Briggs's chest and then shifted her gaze to Kassie herself. "I don't mean to be rude, but it's probably best if you take your hands off my fiancé and take a step back."

Kassie, Briggs's former situationship, blinked at Melissa and then shrugged as she let her hands fall to her sides. "Sorry. I was just a little taken aback." Then she scowled at

Briggs. "A phone call would have been nice. When exactly were you going to tell me you are involved with someone else?"

Briggs opened his mouth to tell her never, but before he could get the word out, his boss, Austin Steele, appeared beside them.

"There you are," Austin said, clasping Briggs on the back. "I'm assuming that Kassie already told you there's been a change with her new album. She liked our work so much she lobbied to record with us again, and the studio wants Kassie's new album ASAP. So we're going to start recording tomorrow. Early. I want to get started by eight. Cool?"

"Um, sure," Briggs said. He worked for Austin at his recording studio, doing the sound mixing on various projects. In fact, that was how he'd met Kassie in the first place. He'd worked on her debut album over a year ago when they'd all been living in Los Angeles. They'd had a short fling before she'd gone out on tour for the past year. But he hadn't known she'd be coming to Keating Hollow to record her next record. He'd just assumed she'd do that in LA again.

"Great." Austin gestured to Kassie. "Since she's staying with you, do your best to make sure she gets to the studio on time, will you? If I recall, Kassie, you're not exactly the most punctual."

"I can't help it if I'm better as a night owl. Most musicians are, Austin." She smiled prettily at him.

"But your voice is better first thing in the morning," he said. "Drink your tea and stay away from dairy."

Briggs was momentarily speechless as he tried to process what he'd just heard. "Austin, I think there's been—"

"Gotta go," Austin said right after his phone buzzed with a text. "We'll talk more in the morning. Brinn's waiting for me." He hurried over to the front door, where his wife was standing, and then they both disappeared outside.

"Why does Austin think you're staying with me?" Briggs demanded, glaring at Kassie.

She shrugged. "Why wouldn't I stay with you? Last year, you said your door was always open the next time I was in town."

"That was when we were in LA. And it wasn't an open invitation to just move in, Kassie," Briggs said tightly.

"You sure seemed welcoming when you were stripping my clothes off every night!" she shot back.

Melissa cleared her throat. "I hate to butt in, but Kassie, I think it's probably best if you get a room at the inn."

Leaning into Melissa, Briggs squeezed her hip in a silent thank you.

"I can't," Kassie said quietly, averting her eyes.

"Why not?" Briggs asked, his tone clipped with irritation. There was no way he was sharing his house with her. Not after the gazillion texts she'd sent after he'd made it clear they weren't going to be an item.

She closed her eyes as she sucked in a sharp breath. "My credit card is maxed out, and the only way the label would let me record up here was if I covered my travel expenses. But since you're here, I figured..." Kassie waved a hand at him. "You didn't seem to have a problem sharing your bed every night before, so I figured I'd surprise you."

Briggs ground his teeth together. There was a reason he'd stopped answering her texts. While he'd thought they were casual, she'd somehow decided that they were in a committed relationship. And when he'd told her he didn't do long distance, she'd just said that they'd see about that. She began texting him every day, updating him on what she was doing. He'd tried to be polite and send short answers in the beginning, but he soon learned that if he gave an inch she'd take a mile, and he'd just stopped answering altogether. If she'd been anyone else, she'd have taken the hint.

But she wasn't. She was Kassie Kinny, an up-and-coming pop star who had started to act like the world should bow at her feet… especially Briggs.

"Last call!" Rhys Silver called from the bar.

"Looks like you have a houseguest, Briggs," Melissa said with a shrug.

"No, I don't. She can't stay with us," he insisted.

Melissa raised one eyebrow and mouthed, *Us?*

"Give us a moment," Briggs said to Kassie as he wrapped his hand around Melissa's wrist and pulled her back toward the hall that led to the restrooms. Once they were out of everyone's earshot, Briggs clasped both of her hands and said, "You can't leave me alone with her."

"What's she going to do, bite?" Melissa shook her head at him. "You're a big boy, Briggs. I'm sure you can handle one houseguest."

"If King was still living with me, then maybe," Briggs said. "He'd be a decent buffer, but with him living with

Sadie now, it's not like I can ask him to come back and... I just can't be alone with her."

"Why? Are you afraid you can't control yourself?" Melissa asked with a look of sheer annoyance on her face. "We're not even dating. It's one thing to pretend to be engaged for an evening, but it's entirely another to have a sleepover. You're asking a bit much, don't you think?"

"I'm asking as a friend, Mel," he said, feeling desperate. "I'm afraid it could turn into some kind of *Fatal Attraction* situation. There's a reason why I begged you to play my fiancée." The moment Kassie had walked into the brewery, he'd impulsively asked Melissa to pretend to be his fiancée, and lucky for him, she'd played along. Now if only he could get her to keep it up for just a little while longer, he might be able to survive Kassie's stay in Keating Hollow.

"So I'd be the one with a boiled bunny on my stove?" she asked, her expression morphing to horrified.

"Oh, come on, Melissa. I'm sure she won't go *that* far. But you just don't understand how relentless this chick is." He whipped out his phone, pulled up her name, and showed Melissa the endless texts that Kassie had sent over the past twelve months. "If I don't have a buffer, she's going to drive me insane."

Melissa took a few seconds to scroll through the texts, and when she looked up at him, her eyes were wide with disbelief. "She sent all of these?"

He nodded. "You heard Austin. She told him she's staying with me. I can't just tell her no when she has nowhere to go. Especially not since I know the studio needs the business. If you'd come stay just long enough for us to find her something else, a short-term rental or something, I'd owe you a huge favor."

"Who's going to pay for the rental?" she asked. "You?"

"Maybe. If I have to." Briggs stared at her in desperation. "Please, Melissa. If she thinks we're really together, I'm pretty sure she'll leave me alone."

Melissa grimaced but then let out a long breath and said, "Fine. But just for tonight. Tomorrow, we figure something else out."

Briggs pulled her into a hug, feeling as if a weight had been lifted off his chest. "You are my new favorite person."

"I bet." She stepped back and smoothed her dress. "Two conditions. I have to stop at my house to get a few things, and you're making breakfast. In bed, preferably."

"Anything you want. I'll stop by the store on the way home, and we'll meet you back at my house. Deal?"

Melissa nodded reluctantly and then muttered, "What have I gotten myself into?"

He ignored the question, grabbed her by the hand, and led her back over to where Kassie was waiting.

The pop star looked at him with a sour expression on her face. "Can we get going? It's been a long day, and all I want to do is soak in a hot bath and then crawl into bed."

Melissa snorted softly as she shook her head.

Kassie ignored her as she stared up at Briggs expectantly.

"We can go, but I have to make a stop on the way home," Briggs said. "You can follow me and then…"

Kassie held out her hand. "I have the address. Just give me a spare key, and I can let myself in."

Melissa let out a bark of humorless laughter before she said, "You're an entitled little thing, aren't you?" Then she turned to Briggs, pressed up onto her tiptoes, and after kissing him on the cheek, she whispered, "Don't cave in to her demands. I'll see you in about a half hour."

Briggs watched as Melissa headed out of the brewery, and then he turned to Kassie. "I'm not giving you a key. You can either go wait for me at the house, or you can follow me to the grocery store. I need to pick up a few things."

"The grocery store? Oh, good idea. I remember how bare your fridge always used to be. Well, unless you counted all the beer that you and King kept on hand. I definitely could use a few things. I'll follow you."

"Suit yourself," he said and then strode out of the brewery, wishing the ground would somehow open up and swallow her whole.

CHAPTER 2

Melissa stared at her overnight bag and shook her head. "What have I gotten myself into?"

The silence in her house was deafening. Normally when she came home, the first thing she'd do was tell Alexa to play one of her many playlists. The music helped her feel less alone. Ever since her mother had moved to Befana Bay a few years ago, she'd found that the silence was a little too much to take. It had just been the two of them when she was growing up, and for some reason, Melissa hadn't ever considered moving out. Why should she? She liked her mom. Other than Sadie, her mom, Rachel, was her best friend. And while she enjoyed her freedom these days, she still missed the company.

Not that she had to worry about that at the moment.

Though she was a little worried about how she'd manage to keep her hands off Briggs. The man was just too yummy for his own good. It really was too bad that she'd promised herself she'd stay away from him. He was a flirt. A man who wasn't one for commitment. And Melissa was looking for a real connection these days. Someone she could come home to every night, who would be there when she got home from one of her work trips. Someone she could count on to help her with the puppy she desperately wanted.

Briggs wasn't that man.

She grabbed her overnight bag and her laptop computer and then strode out of her house. Just as she was putting her roller bag into the back of her Audi SUV, she heard a horn honk. The sound startled her, and she quickly spun but then let out a breath when she saw Sadie climbing out of the new black Toyota Sequoia that King had purchased recently.

"Are you leaving on another trip?" Sadie called as she hurried over.

"No," Melissa said with a nervous laugh. She was a wine rep, and because her territory covered all of Northern California and now the Central Coast, she was often gone for a few days at a time when she was out schmoozing clients. "I'm heading to Briggs's to save him from an overzealous singer who managed to worm her way into staying with him while she records her new album."

"Kassie's here?" King asked with a grimace as he wrapped an arm around Sadie. "And she thinks she's staying with Briggs?"

"Yep." Melissa went on to explain what happened back at the brewery. "So now I'm his buffer, I suppose."

"This is bad. Real bad," King said, shaking his head. He glanced down at Sadie. "You have no idea how crazy this girl is. I think I should probably go over there and let Melissa off the hook."

"No, no," Melissa said quickly as she waved a hand. "That's not necessary. Besides, Kassie already thinks we're engaged. If I don't show up, she's going to find that suspicious." Not to mention that if Kassie realized they'd lied, she'd likely be all over Briggs whether King was there or not. And that just wasn't something she would let happen. "It's fine. It's just for one night. Briggs is gonna find her other accommodations tomorrow."

"That's… nice of you," Sadie said, giving Melissa a cheeky smile as she eyed the overnight bag. "Did you pack that lacy black number you bought last month?"

Melissa glanced at King and then scowled at her friend. "No. I'm not spending the night *with* him, just sleeping over." But as soon as the words were out of her mouth, she had the sinking realization that she probably would be staying in Briggs's room. As his supposed fiancée, sleeping somewhere other than with him would blow their cover.

Sadie chuckled. "Sure, Mel. Call me tomorrow. I'm gonna wanna hear every last detail."

King whipped out his phone, tapped the screen, and then pressed the device to his ear. A moment later, he walked away and said, "Briggs. What the hell is going on?"

Melissa closed the hatchback on her Audi and moved to the driver's side door. "I better get going. When do you two leave again?"

Sadie and King had been spending a lot of time on the road promoting their new single. Melissa missed having her friend right next door all the time, but she was really happy that the new song was doing well. Her friend deserved every good thing that came her way after all she'd been through, losing her mom as a teenager and having a difficult relationship with her absentee father.

"Not for a few weeks," Sadie said. "So we should be around to catch all the fireworks."

"There aren't going to be any fireworks," Melissa said as she climbed into her car. "Don't forget about our dinner plans later this week."

"I won't." Sadie waved and walked over to her house, where King was waiting for her on the porch.

Melissa glanced at the happy couple once more before letting out a sigh and taking off to save Briggs from his crazy stalker.

∼

"THIS IS MY ROOM?" Kassie asked, wrinkling her nose. "There's hardly even a closet in here."

Melissa rolled her eyes so hard she practically gave herself a headache. The princess was not happy with the sleeping arrangements.

"What's wrong with *that* room?" the bratty pop star asked as she pointed to the one across the hall. "It's at least a little bigger and has a nicer bed."

"That's King's room," Briggs said in a flat tone. "It's this or you can have the couch."

"But King isn't here, is he?" Kassie said, making a move to head across the hall.

Briggs stepped in front of her and crossed his arms over

his chest. "No one uses his room but him. It's your choice. The guest room, the couch, or you can find somewhere else to stay."

Kassie pushed her lower lip out in an exaggerated pout, and Melissa wished she could wipe it right off her face. The woman was something else. "Fine," Kassie said with a sigh. "I guess this will do."

"I guess it will," he said and then waited as she hauled in no less than seven suitcases.

"How long are you planning to be here?" Melissa asked, wondering how she'd managed to fit it all into the compact Mazda SUV that was parked outside. It was one of those vehicles that had a back seat, but no one over five feet tall was going to be happy riding in it.

"As long as it takes," Kassie said with a huff and then glared at Briggs. "You could have helped me haul my luggage in here."

"I already brought it inside. The rest is up to you." Briggs wrapped his arm around Melissa's shoulders and added, "Mel and I are going to bed. Be up and ready to go by 7:30."

"What? Austin said we didn't need to be there until eight!" she whined.

"Right. We need time to get into town. Be up and ready to go or else I'll be dragging you out of here." Without another word, he guided Melissa into his room and slammed the door behind him.

She dropped her overnight bag onto a chair in the corner and then stood there, staring at him slumped against the door and wondering what to do next.

"Zeus above," Briggs muttered to himself.

Melissa chuckled. "Are you praying to the Greek god?"

"Yes." He raised his gaze to hers. "How did this happen?"

"You were too much of a coward to tell her to stop texting you, and now you're stuck with her… at least for tonight." Melissa walked over to him, took his hand in hers, and then led him over to the bed. "Sit."

He did as he was told and was silent as he watched her climb onto the bed and position herself behind him.

"You need to relax a little," Melissa said as she started to massage his shoulders. "It's just for one night, right? Tomorrow she'll be out of here, and you'll only have to deal with her at work."

He let out a grunt. "Only at work. You're not really familiar with how recording works, are you?"

"I only know what Sadie's told me," she said. "I know she spent a lot of time with King, trying to get it right. But if I recall correctly, they didn't spend more than a few days in the studio."

"That's… not typical," he said and let out a low moan when she dug into a knot right at the base of his neck. "That's perfect. Keep doing that."

Melissa dug her thumb into the muscles, feeling an intense sense of satisfaction with each noise he made. She liked having the power to make him feel that good. "You were saying that King and Sadie's process isn't typical…"

"Oh, yeah. Those two have something magical."

"Quite literally," Melissa added. When Sadie sang with King, her magic blossomed and she was able to manipulate emotions. It was both awesome and somewhat terrifying, especially when she hadn't known she was doing it. But she had it under control now, and the two of them together made the most beautiful music.

"Right. That means that when they work together, something just clicks. It's a sixth sense. For most other artists, they go into the studio with a song or idea, and we end up having them trying it out two dozen different ways. The process can mean extremely long hours. The last time when we worked on Kassie's debut record, we often were in the studio well into the night. When things start to look promising, no one wants to leave because you never know if the next day will yield the same results. So for the next however many weeks or months, I'll be spending a significant amount of time with Kassie Kinny whether I like it or not."

"No wonder you're so tense," Melissa said, feeling a little bit sorry for him. If she had to spend that kind of time with someone who was so manipulative, she'd lose her mind.

"The massage is helping," he said with a contented sigh. "You're really saving the day here, Melissa. You know that, right?"

"I do," she said, smiling to herself. The truth was she really liked Briggs. If she was only looking for a good time, she'd be ready to fall into his arms for the night. She didn't have a moral objection to a casual relationship. It was just that she was ready for more. Seeing her best friend fall in love with King had triggered something in her. She was tired of coming home to an empty house. To not having a special someone to call each night when she was traveling for work. And if she let herself get involved with Briggs, she was going to want more than he was able to give. So friends were all they could be to each other.

She could do that.

Right?

Wrong.

Briggs turned to look at her, and the interest in his heated gaze was enough to make her forget everything she'd just been thinking.

He reached up and brushed a lock of hair out of her eyes and said, "How about I return the favor?"

Before she could answer, he repositioned himself so that he was sitting against his headboard with his feet out in front of him. He tapped his thigh and said, "Put your feet here."

"You're going to give me a foot massage?" she asked, completely caught off guard.

"Yep. You're on your feet a lot. In heels, right?"

She nodded.

"Well, let me ease some of that tension. It's the least I can do after you've gone through all this trouble." He gave her that wicked half smile that never failed to make her want to throw herself at him. But thankfully she wasn't so far gone that she just pounced on him. Instead, she did as he asked and propped herself up on a pillow as she tucked her feet into his lap. "You're probably going to regret this since I've been on my feet all day."

"I can handle it," he said as he reached into his nightstand and pulled out a bottle of lotion.

She raised one eyebrow at him, refusing to voice the thoughts in her head.

He just laughed and said, "Get your mind out of the gutter. There's nothing wrong with men moisturizing."

"Of course not," she said with a laugh.

Then, as Briggs doused his hands with the lotion, suddenly the lights in the bedroom dimmed and a few candles that were sitting on his dresser flickered to life, the flames casting a warm glow.

Melissa glanced around and then stared at Briggs. "Did you do that? Are you an air witch or fire witch?" It was unusual for a witch to have the ability to both manipulate objects and light fires.

"Technically, I'm both," he said with a shrug. "I'm actually an elemental witch."

"Wow," she said softly. "Air, water, fire, and earth. That's impressive."

"Not really. When I was younger all it did was get me into trouble. A lot of trouble. It was better if I didn't use my magic at all. These days, I really only use it when I want to seduce a gorgeous woman."

"Is that what you're trying to do? Seduce me?" Melissa knew she should be backing away, putting distance between them, but with his warm hands already easing the tension in her feet, she couldn't bring herself to move even an inch. His touch was just too delicious.

"Is it working?" he teased.

"Yes," she answered honestly. What would be the harm? Just one night. It wasn't like she'd never had a one-night stand before.

His hands froze on her foot as he stared at her intently.

After a moment, he shook his head and climbed off the bed. "We shouldn't. Not like this."

Melissa frowned at him. "Not like what?"

"This." He waved his hand around the room and then waved at the door. "You're here doing me a favor, and I'm… Well, I guess I'm going to take a cold shower. You said before that we were just sleeping, and I don't want to make you regret helping me out."

"I won't regret it," she said even as he disappeared into the bathroom.

Melissa flopped back onto the bed and stared up at the ceiling. She honestly didn't know if she should be relieved or offended. Briggs had done nothing but flirt with her since he'd moved to town. And now that she was ready to let her guard down and have a little fun, he was acting all chivalrous?

"Ugh," she groaned and covered her face with both hands. Why were men so confusing?

Melissa rose from the bed, rummaged around in her overnight bag, and found her pink silk pajamas that she'd brought and her toiletry case. Then she stood in the middle of the room, wondering what to do. If she went to use the spare bathroom, no doubt Kassie would wonder why. She'd either have to wait until Briggs was done or…

The bathroom door wasn't quite closed, and when she took a closer look, she realized that the shower was behind a closed door and the sink was free to use. She quickly brushed her teeth, washed her face, and got into her pajamas. Then she slipped into bed and decided that when

Briggs appeared from the shower, she'd be the one to do the seducing.

CHAPTER 3

Briggs wanted nothing more than to climb into the bed next to Melissa, rip the Kindle out of her hands, and ravish her until the sun came up. He'd been fantasizing about having her in his bed for months now. The gorgeous brunette with a sassy tongue was just his type. It didn't hurt that she didn't care one bit about the music business.

When he'd been back in LA, it seemed that every woman he'd dated had thought he'd be a one-way ticket to a recording deal. That was part of the reason why he'd started hooking up with Kassie. She already had a deal and hadn't been looking to him to help her in her career.

Not that he had connections to help someone anyway. He was just a sound mixer. Sure, he was best friends with King McGrath, but that didn't mean he had producers and managers on speed dial. Everything was just so transactional in that town. Keating Hollow was about as opposite of that life as one could get.

The town settled him. There was something about it that just felt right. Sort of like Melissa.

He shoved all thoughts of impropriety out of his mind and went to his closet, where he found a couple of extra blankets and a pillow.

"What are you doing with those?" Melissa asked as she placed her Kindle on the bedside table.

"Making a bed on the floor."

"Why?" she asked, confusion written all over her pretty face.

"Because it's the chivalrous thing to do," he said, still clutching the blankets.

She snorted. "Chivalrous my ass. Put those away and just get in bed. We are both adults. There's no reason for you to sleep on the floor."

He opened his mouth to argue but was cut off when there was a sharp knock on the door.

"Briggs, it's too cold in here," Kassie said as she barged into the room without an invitation. "You need to change the thermostat. If I'm freezing all night, my voice will be like ass tomorrow." She frowned, staring at him and his pile of blankets. "What are you doing with those?"

"Kassie, what the hell do you think you're doing?" he barked, unable to believe that she'd just barged into the room.

"I'm trying to make sure I can sing tomorrow. Austin isn't going to be too happy if I show up with a frog in my throat." Kassie glanced at Melissa. "That's what you wear to bed when you're sleeping with a man like Briggs?"

Melissa glanced down at her pink silk pajamas and frowned. "What's wrong with this?"

Kassie rolled her eyes, walked up to Briggs, took the blankets, and said, "Raise the thermostat two degrees. With these blankets, I should be comfortable enough." Then she swept out of the room like she was the queen of the castle.

"Well, I guess that settles it," Melissa said.

"Settles what?" he asked as he glared at the door, unable to keep his ire in check. His fingers curled into fists, and suddenly magic started to spark over his skin just like it used to when it flared out of control. "Son of a—"

"Whoa," Melissa said from right behind him, and she placed her hands on his shoulders.

The magic vanished right along with the pressure in his chest. He let out a breath and then turned to stare down at her. "How did you do that?"

"Do what?" she asked.

"The magic. You made it disappear."

"I—that's not... I don't know what you mean," she stammered. "I'm not magical. Like, at all."

He shook his head slowly and then pulled her into his arms, hugging her. "Maybe not, but what you just did was pure magic."

She let out a nervous chuckle. "What does that mean?"

He let her go and then led her back to the bed. "Did you see the magic sparking over my skin?"

"Yes," she said. "I wasn't sure what you were planning, but I figured whatever it was, you probably shouldn't do it while you were mad. I was just trying to get you to slow down a minute."

"You made it disappear. Your touch. That magic was out of control. I didn't call it up," he explained.

She blinked at him.

Briggs held her dark gaze for a long moment and then sucked in a deep breath. It was time to explain. "The reason I rarely used my magic before is because I wasn't good at controlling it. That's why I was always getting into trouble. Serious trouble. Eventually, I decided that if I didn't want to end up arrested by the Magical Task Force I'd have to give up magic altogether."

"But you used it tonight with the lights and the candles," she said.

"I did. That's because there's something about Keating Hollow that settles me. The magic of the town, the people, the fresh air. I'm not really sure, but it's one of the only places on earth where I can use magic without it controlling me. Or at least it was until Kassie just barged in here. But then you touched me and the magic disappeared, so it looks like you just saved me again… or rather saved Kassie from goddess knows what."

"She'd look awesome with a pimple right between her eyes," Melissa said, her eyes glinting with mischief. "Maybe I should have kept my hands to myself."

Briggs chuckled as he shook his head. "Please don't."

She let her gaze roam over his chest. And when she licked her lips, he egged her on by tugging off the tight T-shirt he was wearing just before he climbed onto the bed.

Heat flashed in her eyes, and that was all he needed to know.

"Come here," he said, his voice rough as he reached for her, tugging her so that she rolled on top of him.

"Well, this is a far cry from sleeping in a nest on the floor," she said, her voice just as rough as his.

"Yeah, that's not happening." He buried his hand into her thick dark hair and then whispered, "Kiss me, Melissa."

She let out a soft sigh and then pressed her warm lips against his.

They paused in that moment, just breathing each other in. Briggs felt his skin prickle with a different kind of magic. The kind that touched his soul. That kind that told him whatever this thing was between them, it wasn't just a one-night stand. It was something much, much more. And although that knowledge normally would have scared the daylights out of him, all he felt in that moment was a *rightness* he'd never felt before.

And when Melissa finally darted her tongue out to taste him, he closed his eyes, wrapped his arms around her, and made it his mission to explore every inch of the amazing creature who'd save him not once, but twice that night. He was going to make it worth her while even if it took him all night.

BRIGGS WOKE the next morning with his arms wrapped around Melissa. Her head was nestled on his shoulder, and her vanilla scent was intoxicating. He trailed his fingers down her bare arm and wished they had all morning to spend together. If he'd had his way, he'd call in to work and spend the next few hours doing his damnedest to coax those sweet moans out of her again and again and again.

"It's early," she mumbled as she burrowed into him.

"I promised someone breakfast in bed." He pressed a kiss to her temple.

She tilted her head up and opened one eye. "You're really going to make me breakfast in bed?"

"A promise is a promise."

Melissa rose over him and gave him a long lingering kiss. When she finally pulled away, Briggs was breathless and moments away from ravaging her again. But then his alarm went off and he groaned.

She flopped back onto the bed and said, "Dammit."

"You can say that again." He pressed a kiss to her palm and then rolled out of bed.

"I have to say, the view here is stunning," Melissa said.

Briggs glanced at his window and frowned when he saw that the shades were still drawn. But when he shifted his gaze to her and saw her staring at him with open admiration, he couldn't help the smile that tugged at his lips. "Right back at ya."

He pulled on a pair of shorts and his T-shirt from the night before and then went for the door. "How do you take your coffee?"

"With an IV," she deadpanned.

"A woman after my own heart. Black?"

She nodded.

"Okay. I'll be back."

"I'll be waiting."

The innuendo in her tone almost had him hightailing it back to the bed, but when he heard the water from the guest bathroom, he knew that Kassie was up, and that was enough to throw a wet blanket on his libido.

He made his way into the kitchen, made a pot of coffee and a batch of waffles. And because he was feeling generous, he made enough for Kassie, too. He placed hers in a warm oven and then took a full breakfast tray into the bedroom.

Melissa was sitting up, staring at her phone. The minute he walked in, she looked up, and her eyes widened when she saw the tray of food. "You made homemade waffles?"

"Don't sound so surprised," he said. "Were you expecting something out of the freezer?"

She chuckled softly. "I honestly don't know what I was expecting, but it wasn't this."

He placed the tray beside her and then kissed her on the cheek. "Enjoy. I'm going to get in the shower."

When he emerged from the bathroom fifteen minutes later, Melissa beamed at him. "The only thing more enjoyable than last night is this coffee." She took a sip and added, "Keep this up and I might actually marry you for real."

A ripple of pleasure washed over him as his lips twitched into a small smile. And for just the briefest second, he imagined her in a sexy formfitting wedding dress walking down the aisle toward him.

Where in the world had that come from? He frowned and shook his head, suddenly unsettled.

"What's wrong?" she asked.

"Nothing. I just need to get moving. Take however much time you need and lockup on your way out."

"It's because I said I'd marry you, isn't it?" She let out a sigh. "It was just a figure of speech. For the love of the gods, don't go all man on me."

"It wasn't that. I swear," he said, walking back over to the bed and carefully sitting next to her. Then he placed both of his hands on her cheeks and leaned in, kissing her so thoroughly that they were both breathless when he released her. "Thank you for pretending to be my fiancée last night. Can I take you out to dinner tonight as a thank you?"

She looked flustered as she stared at him. "Dinner?"

"Yeah. How about that new place, the Elegant Cauldron? I hear they have the best lasagna within three counties. That's what Miss Maple said, anyway," he added with a wink, referring to the woman who owned A Spoon Full of Magic, the magical bakery in the heart of Keating Hollow.

"Well, if Miss Maple said it, then it must be true," she said.

"It's a date then," he said. "I'll get us reservations for seven o'clock and pick you up at twenty till."

As Briggs walked out of his room, he smiled to himself, anticipating getting to see Melissa again that night, and maybe, just maybe, she'd find her way back to his bed.

He knocked on Kassie's door. "Time to go."

Her door flung open, and she stood there in a short skirt, knee-high boots, and a sparkling top. She looked as if she were getting ready to go on stage and put on a live show. "I need to eat breakfast first."

"There's coffee in the pot and a warm waffle in the

oven," he said. "There's an insulated cup in the cupboard you can use. You can eat the waffle on your way."

She stared at him like he'd grown three heads. "Are you being serious right now? I can't have coffee and a waffle."

"Why not?" he asked, frowning at her.

"I need tea and honey for my voice. And pop stars *do not* eat waffles." She stomped past him down the hall and into the kitchen. "Please tell me you have fresh fruit and salmon."

"Salmon?" he asked as he followed her. "There's fruit. Apples and oranges are in the basket. I thought you got groceries while we were at the store last night."

"I did get some things, like my tea and honey, but I was tired and forgot to get breakfast stuff." She made a show of opening all his cabinets and huffing as she didn't find whatever she needed. Then she pulled a tea bag out of her pocket and said, "Please tell me you have an electric kettle."

That he did have. Or at least King did. "It's right next to the coffee pot." He gestured to the machine. "And there's honey in the cabinet above it."

"Thank the gods you aren't totally useless. You'd think since you lived with a singer that you'd know these things."

The only thing he knew was that King never ate dairy before singing. Everything else was pretty much on the table. And he'd certainly never refused Briggs's waffles.

She huffed while she made her tea, sliced up an apple, and grabbed a handful of almonds. "Let's go," she said once she had her tea in one of his thermal mugs. "We don't want to be late."

"We certainly don't," he said and followed her out of the

house. Once they were in his truck, he said, "We'll look for alternative housing for you on our lunch break."

She spit out her tea and sputtered, "What?"

"Look, Kassie. You can't stay with me. It's just not going to work out. So we're going to see if we can get you a short-term rental or something," he said.

"Did you miss the part about me not having any room on my credit card?" she nearly shrieked.

"No, I didn't miss it. We'll figure something out. You can pay me back when you start to make the big bucks or something."

"I'm not taking your charity," she said, her voice suddenly cold.

"But you'll invade my house for however long this takes?" he asked, casting her a look of irritation. "It's this or nothing. Understand?"

"And when I tell Austin that you took advantage of me?" she threatened.

Magic burst like flames over Briggs's skin, and suddenly the truck lost power. He gripped the steering wheel tight and eased the truck off the road. Once they'd stopped, he stared straight ahead, breathing deeply while he willed himself to get control of his rage. When he finally spoke, he said, "Looks like we're going to be late after all."

CHAPTER 4

Melissa had just stepped out of the shower and was dripping wet when her phone rang in the other room. She wrapped a towel around herself, padded into the bedroom, and was surprised to see Briggs's name flashing across the screen. "Miss me already?" she asked in as sultry a tone as she could muster.

"My truck broke down. I've already called the tow truck, but is there any way you can come get us and give us a ride to the studio?"

"Oof. That sucks. What happened?" She walked over to the chair where she'd left her overnight bag and pulled out her jeans and T-shirt.

There was a slight pause before he said, "I don't know. Just lost power. Now we're stranded. Do you have time to pick us up? If not, I can call King. It's just that you're closer and we're already late."

"Of course I can. Give me two minutes to put some clothes on."

When he didn't respond to the fact that she was still naked, she knew he was in no mood for flirting. After a few beats he said, "Thanks, Melissa."

"No problem. Text me with your location and I'll get there as soon as possible." She ended the call, and while she was yanking her jeans on, her phone pinged with a text. It first had the nearest cross street and then Briggs had added, *hurry before my magic flares out of control and Kassie ends up roadkill.*

Melissa let out a bark of laughter. But then she recalled how angry he was the night before and how he'd only calmed because of her touch, and she wondered how much truth was in that text. She rushed to finish getting dressed and then ran out of the house.

Ten minutes later, she pulled to a stop behind his truck. The tow truck was there, and Billy from Hollow Towing was already hooking the truck up to winch it onto the flatbed. "Hey, cowboy. Need a ride?" she called out the window at Briggs.

He walked over with his shoulders hunched and stress lines etched around his eyes.

"You look like you've aged five years in the last half hour," she said softly. "What happened?"

"I think I short-circuited my truck," he said.

"How?" She stared at the truck as if it held any answers.

"My magic flared out of control." He gritted his teeth as he glared in Kassie's direction.

The singer was standing next to the tow truck, holding

her phone out as she documented the morning, explaining to all of her followers that she was going to be late to her first day of recording the new album because her ride broke down. She pouted for the camera and then rattled off an address ID where her followers could send money to 'buy her a coffee.' She promised them a personal shout out once she got the notification.

"That's it for now. Can you believe we have to walk the rest of the way into town? But anything for my devoted fans. It's all for you." She gave an exaggerated wink and then logged off.

"Walk into town?" Melissa repeated.

Briggs shook his head. "Welcome to the world of LA influencers."

"Was she like this when you were with her back in LA?" Melissa asked out of morbid curiosity. She just couldn't imagine Briggs being interested in a woman like that.

"No. At least not like that. She posted a lot on social media, but that's to be expected from someone trying to break out in the music industry. But the lying and over-the-top antics? That's definitely new."

"It's not a lie, Briggs," Kassie snapped. "We broke down, and I'm just sharing it with my fans. So what if I stretched the truth a little? No one wants to hear that your *fiancée* is picking us up and we'll be at work in ten minutes. They want drama. Why else do you think they follow me?"

"For the music?" he muttered under his breath.

"I heard that!" she called and then took a selfie with Billy, the tow truck guy.

He groaned. "I need to go talk to Billy for a minute. I'll

be right back and then we can get going." Briggs took a few steps but then stopped and turned back to her. "I'm not making you late for anything, am I?"

Melissa shook her head. "No. I have work to do, but no appointments this morning. It's all paperwork. Don't worry, I wasn't exactly getting the fastest start this morning anyway."

He grinned, knowing exactly why she'd lounged around in bed. Then he nodded and went to talk to the tow truck driver.

The front passenger door opened and Kassie climbed in. She leaned back against the seat and closed her eyes as she let out a heavy sigh.

"Rough morning?" Melissa asked.

"Rough week. This is just the cherry on top of the crap pile." The woman, who looked like she was ready to step right into a music video, turned to look at Melissa and then at Briggs, who was still talking to Billy. "A word of warning. Watch out for that one. He has anger management issues."

So far, the only time Melissa had seen Briggs acting any way other than relaxed or cheerful was when Kassie was around. And she had to say, she understood why he was so upset. The woman had walked into his life without warning and completely disrupted it with her demands. If Briggs's magic really had flared out of control and killed his truck, she had no doubt that the woman sitting next to her had provoked him. "I can take care of myself."

"Famous last words." She went back to staring into her phone and then started tapping on the screen.

Billy climbed into his tow truck and started to haul the truck away while Briggs returned to Melissa's SUV. He spotted Kassie in the front passenger seat and Melissa could see the irritation roll through him. But he didn't say a word as he climbed into the back and said, "Thanks for waiting. I appreciate it."

Melissa glanced in the rearview mirror, smiled, and said, "Ready?"

Kassie let out a giant sigh and said, "Of course he is. We're *late*."

"Oh, is that right?" Melissa asked with a chuckle as she met Briggs's eyes in the mirror. "I would have never guessed."

Briggs smiled at her, and the tension seemed to melt off him.

"Ugh. Stop flirting. You're making me nauseous," Kassie said.

"You think that's flirting?" Melissa asked. "Dating in LA must be like living in another world." She eased her SUV back onto the road and sped down the highway.

"It's a lot better than this boring town. Imagine needing to call someone to pick you up instead of just ordering a ride-share. Talk about living in the Dark Ages," she said and then turned to stare out the window.

Melissa didn't say anything. Part of the reason she loved Keating Hollow was because there was always someone to call. Someone who would help out at a moment's notice. They didn't need ride-shares. And no one she knew lived the majority of their lives online. There was a reason there was a housing shortage in Keating Hollow. People rarely moved away, and it had become a haven for magical creatives who'd gotten tired of the hamster wheel of Hollywood.

But she had a hard time imagining Kassie ever appreciating the magic of Keating Hollow. At least that meant she'd disappear once she was done recording her album, and hopefully Briggs wouldn't have to deal with her again.

"Good thing I was here considering your credit card is maxed out. I don't know of any ride-shares that work for free," Melissa said flippantly.

Briggs let out a chortle before belatedly trying to cover it with a cough.

To Melissa's surprise, Kassie didn't deliver any sort of biting comeback. She just glared at her and then went back to staring out the window.

A few minutes later, Melissa pulled up in front of the recording studio. As Briggs and Kassie exited the vehicle, she called out, "Have a good day, kids!"

Kassie stomped inside while Briggs lingered for a moment at her open window.

"Need a ride home?" she asked.

"That would be great. But if it's too much trouble, I can ask King. I'm sure he wouldn't mind," Briggs said.

"I'll be around. Just text me. I still need to pick up my stuff from your house anyway. I hurried out of there so fast that all I managed to grab was my pocketbook and laptop."

"You're the best." Briggs leaned down and gave her a kiss on the cheek. "Thanks… for everything."

"Anytime," she said before she could think it through and then felt her face heat as she blushed furiously.

He chuckled softly. "I'll remember that."

Melissa watched as the man swaggered into the studio, and she knew she was doomed.

THE INTOXICATING scent of nutmeg and cinnamon made Melissa's mouth water as she walked into Incantation Café. It was a clear, crisp, January day in Keating Hollow and she just didn't want to spend it cooped up in the office in her house. Instead, she decided to plant herself near a window at the enchanted café while overloading herself with caffeine.

"Good morning," Hanna Pelsh-Silver said as she paused at Melissa's table. She eyed the laptop that was already open. "Work day?"

"Yep, but I just wanted to enjoy this nice day a little. You don't mind if I take up a table, do you? I'm gonna need the largest latte you have."

Hanna chuckled. "Of course not. Did you want pumpkin loaf to go with it? A fresh batch just came out of the oven."

As much as Melissa wanted to say yes, she shook her head. Hanna knew how much she loved it, but after the waffles that morning, there was barely going to be room for the latte. "Maybe later. I think the latte is good for now."

"You got it." Hanna hurried off while Melissa went to work answering emails and setting up visits to the accounts she serviced up and down the coast. She was a wine rep for various cottage wineries from all over Northern California. She loved her job and took pride in making sure that there was always a healthy demand for the wineries she repped.

Two lattes and two hours later, the bell above the door rang and a shadow fell over Melissa's table. "Are these seats taken?"

Melissa glanced up to see Sadie and Imogen Thane standing over her. She grinned at them. "They are now."

The two women took their seats. Hanna arrived again and took their coffee orders. And then once Hanna was gone, Sadie leaned in and said, "Tell me everything."

"Everything what?" Imogen asked.

Imogen Thane was the event planner at the Pelsh winery, and Melissa had become friendly with her through their connection.

"I spent the night at Briggs's last night," Melissa said, choosing to just come out with it. If she couldn't tell her friends, what was the point, right?

Imogen raised both eyebrows. "I thought you were looking for Mr. Right, not Mr. Right now."

"I am, but…" She shrugged. "He needed me to do him a favor, and then one thing led to another and…"

"You slept with him, didn't you?" Sadie said with a gleam in her eyes. "How was it?"

"Sadie," Melissa said as she glanced around the café. "I'm not one to kiss and tell."

"Since when?" Sadie challenged.

Melissa didn't even have an argument. It was true that she pretty much told Sadie everything. They had been best friends forever, after all. But this time, she wasn't sure she wanted to share the details. That was something that was just between her and Briggs. "Let's just say we had a nice night and leave it at that."

Sadie narrowed her eyes at her. "How nice of a night?"

"A very nice night," Melissa relented. "But it was just one night. Now it's done. Briggs won't need me as a buffer anymore, and everything can go back to the way it was before."

"You mean before you agreed to be his fake fiancée because his ex-situationship showed up? The one that will be here for a few months? Because you don't think he's going to pull on that thread again?" Sadie asked.

"Whoa. Wait just a minute," Imogen demanded, waving her hands in the air, making her dark curly blond hair bounce around her face. "I feel like I missed something."

Melissa quickly explained the situation and then picked up her phone to search Kassie's social media. Once she was on her IG page, she handed the phone to Imogen. "This is who he's dealing with. You can see why he panicked and begged me to help him out."

Imogen shook her head. "Why are some men like this? He's the type who'll sleep with anyone, and then when they turn out to be more than he can handle, he turns to another woman to save him."

"Isn't that the truth," Melissa said. "But he claims she wasn't this bad before she started getting a taste of fame. I suppose I can believe that. Fame does weird things to some people."

"Yeah it does," Sadie said. "Thankfully, King is only really interested in the music, not being chased by every crazed fan that recognizes him."

Melissa shuddered slightly as she remembered the women who had practically stalked King all over town not that long ago. Why anyone would want to live like that was beyond her.

"Listen, now that King and I are going to be in town for a while, I was thinking maybe we could plan a group get-together. Card night maybe?" Sadie asked. "All this traveling has really made me miss home and everyone here. I just want to spend as much time as possible doing normal things. What do you two think? Are you in?"

Melissa beamed at her. "I'd love that. Who else would you invite?"

"I was thinking Grayson and Amelia." Sadie turned to Imogen. "You and Shaun of course. If your sister and Cash are around, they'd be welcome, too. And then there's Briggs. Can't leave him out."

Melissa groaned. "Awkward."

"You said the night went well," Sadie countered. "Come on. He's King's best friend. I can't just have a card night and not invite him."

"I suppose," Melissa said, though her cheeks were already heating with embarrassment. What if Briggs acted like nothing happened? Or worse, brought someone with him? She pushed the thoughts out of her head and asked, "Where are you gonna host this shindig? Your place? Your table only sits six people."

"I can host," Imogen said. "I've got a recipe for a stew that will feed an army. And there's plenty of space at my new place. I've been wanting to do a test run in the refurbished barn that I plan to rent out for events." Imogen had recently put a down payment on a small house on the edge of town that came with five acres and a barn that she'd been working to renovate for event space. As an event planner, it was the perfect property for her.

Melissa and Sadie shared a quick look, and then they both nodded and said, "Yes!"

Imogen laughed. "That didn't take much convincing."

Sadie shrugged. "Neither of us are exactly the best cooks. But we're really good at desserts. Let us handle that, okay?"

"You're on," Imogen said.

Melissa sat back in her chair, thoroughly enjoying the impromptu meetup with her friends. It wasn't often she got to do this. With her work schedule and Sadie out on the road so often, performing her new song, she'd been spending a lot of time on her couch. Some girl time was exactly what she needed.

After chatting and laughing for an hour, Sadie looked at her watch and said, "I know we've been downing the coffee, but is anyone ready for a real lunch?"

"I am," Melissa said, her stomach rumbling at the mere thought of actual food. Her waffle was long gone.

"I'm in. Where to?" Imogen asked.

"Mystyk Pizza?" Sadie asked. "I am absolutely craving their pesto chicken and olive pizza. I don't know what they put in that sauce, but my mouth is watering just thinking about it."

"Mystyk Pizza it is," Imogen said as she stood. "They have the best cheese bread within a hundred miles."

"You can say that again," Melissa said. "We'll probably need a double order."

"But what will you two eat?" Sadie teased as she threw some money on the table for a tip.

Melissa did the same, and her heart was full as she followed her two friends out of the café.

CHAPTER 5

"Pizza?" Kassie complained as she followed Briggs into Mystyk Pizza. "You expect me to eat that and then go sing later?"

"You don't have to follow me," Briggs grumbled. "There are other restaurants on this street. The Cozy Cave is right over there. The brewery isn't that far. Or if you want your tea, Incantation Café is close by too. But if that's too much trouble for you, this place does have salads."

She sighed heavily. "I suppose salad is fine. As long as the dressing isn't full of fat."

"You'd have to ask the server," he said, trying to keep the irritation out of his tone. They'd had a slow start that morning. First they'd been late due to the truck breaking down, then there'd been an equipment issue. Finally, when they'd gotten around to putting down the tracks of Kassie's first song, she and Austin had butted heads on the production. Kassie wanted to sing it as an up-tempo pop song, while Austin thought it was better as a soft, stripped-down version.

Briggs usually didn't get involved during the creative stage. He was the tech guy who sat behind the boards and tried his damnedest to give the client what they were looking for. But Kassie kept pulling him into it and demanding his opinion.

He hadn't been amused. And even less so when he'd had to side with her. The song was good both ways, but the upbeat, poppy version sounded like the kind of song that would get a lot of air play.

That was when Austin had glared at him and then kicked them out for lunch and said they'd regroup when they got back. Briggs didn't particularly enjoy pissing off his boss.

"Hey, look who's here," a familiar voice said from behind Briggs.

He turned and spotted Sadie, Imogen Thane, and Melissa. A smile stretched across his face as he stared at Melissa, remembering how it felt to wake up with her in his arms.

"Perfect. Just perfect," Kassie muttered.

Briggs ignored her and went over to slip his arm around Melissa's shoulders and brush a kiss across her cheek. "Are you stalking me?" he teased.

"You wish," she said, leaning into him.

He tightened his grip on her and said a silent prayer to the gods for saving him from having to spend his lunch hour alone with Kassie Kinny.

"A table for five?" the waiter asked as he started grabbing menus.

"Yes," Briggs said before anyone else could chime in.

"Right this way." The waiter took off, weaving through the tables.

Briggs released Melissa but placed his hand on the small of her back as he led her through the restaurant.

She leaned in. "Looks like we arrived just in time."

"I owe you big," he whispered.

"I'll collect later." She smirked at him.

He'd make certain of it.

"Okay, lovebirds," Sadie called, humor dancing in her eyes. "That's enough. Some of us are here to eat."

Kassie sat in the chair at the end of the table and turned so that she wasn't facing any of them.

Briggs knew that meant she was uncomfortable, but he made no effort to try and sooth her ruffled feathers. She'd barged into his life the night before like a Tasmanian devil with zero care for how it affected him. If she wanted to remove herself from the situation, she could just get up and leave.

They all took their seats, and after they ordered, Imogen turned to Kassie. "So, I hear you're a singer."

Kassie nodded. "Yeah. I'm here making an album."

"That's exciting. I'll have to look you up." Imogen pulled her phone out and started tapping on it. A moment later, she said, "There you are. I just added your previous album to my playlist. I'll check it out on my way to my afternoon appointment."

Kassie perked up and beamed at her. "That's so nice. I hope you like it."

"Me, too," Imogen said.

"What event are you working on now?" Melissa asked Imogen.

Briggs sat back and listened to the conversation, feeling slightly ashamed. It hadn't taken much at all for Imogen to coax out a human response from Kassie, though Briggs had noted that she'd done it by appealing to her ego. Still, if he wanted to get through the next weeks or months of working with her, he should probably learn to find a way to smooth her edges.

"A birthday party for Miss Maple's niece. As you can imagine, she has a lot of surprises in store," Imogen said.

"You plan kids' birthday parties?" Kassie asked her, looking slightly horrified.

Briggs could relate to Kassie's reaction. While he liked kids fine, he couldn't imagine having to wrangle an entire party of them.

Imogen chuckled. "Yes, among other things. I'm actually a wedding planner, but I do other events to supplement my income."

"Oh." She cast a quick glance at Briggs before averting her eyes. "I guess you're planning their wedding then, too?"

Briggs opened his mouth to say they hadn't started any planning yet, but Sadie cut him off.

"Yes. Isn't it great? We just spent all morning at Incantation Café going over the details." Sadie clutched at Melissa's arm. "I can't wait to plan the bachelorette party."

Melissa glared at her friend, and Briggs instantly knew

that Sadie was putting on a show for Kassie. They hadn't done any planning. Sadie just wanted to needle the singer.

He was all in for that plan. He grinned at Sadie as he said, "You and King will have to coordinate the date so that my bachelor party is the same night."

Melissa gave him a wide-eyed look, and he had to bite his cheek to keep from laughing.

"Did you decide on a venue? How about the entertainment?" Briggs asked Melissa. "Are Sadie and King singing?"

"Now that's a perfect idea!" Sadie exclaimed, having way too much fun with the fake wedding. "Maybe we'll even write you lovebirds your own song."

"Stop," Melissa said, chuckling. "Now you're just being too much."

"It's never too much for my bestie," Sadie teased.

"Right," Melissa said dryly. "Did you already set up an appointment at Magic and Lace?"

"Oh my goddess, did you see that new dress they have in the display window, Mels?" Sadie asked. "It's perfect for you. Just perfect."

Melissa's expression softened as she smiled wistfully. "Yeah, I did. It's like an updated version of the one my grandmother is wearing in that old photo I have."

As Briggs watched her, he suddenly had a vision of her walking down the aisle… toward him. The flutter of anticipation that rippled through his chest was enough to sober him. Was he really having thoughts of marrying Melissa? He swallowed the lump in his throat and lightly coughed.

"Uh-oh," Melissa said, her eyes twinkling. "I think we might be freaking him out. Quick, someone change the subject before I end up with a runaway groom."

"Very funny," Briggs muttered.

"Kassie," Imogen said, turning to her. "Where are you staying while you're in town? Did you find a room at the inn? Or did you decide to go with a short-term rental?"

"Neither, I'm staying with Briggs. We're… old friends," Kassie said.

"Oh, I thought…" Imogen trailed off as she looked between Briggs and Kassie.

Briggs felt his blood pressure rise. The very idea of spending even another night with her under his roof made his entire body tense. He'd never make it if he had to spend all day and every night with her around. She was just too much for him. He'd lose his ever-loving mind. He stared Kassie down as he spoke. "We were going to find her alternate accommodations over lunch."

"Is that what we were going to do?" Kassie shot back. "What about my… ah, limited funds issue."

"We'll work it out," he said. "I already said you can pay me back when the big bucks start to roll in."

Melissa, Sadie, and Imogen watched the debate like they were at a tennis match.

All three of them were staring at Kassie when she said, "I won't take a handout. Especially from you. Not after the way you just ghosted me."

"And mooching off my hospitality isn't taking a handout?" he shot back. "It's a loan. Not a handout."

"I've already moved in. There's no need to move again.

I'm perfectly fine where I am. Even if I do have to listen to your pathetic porno moans all night."

Briggs's magic was back, zapping through his veins, making him feel as if he were going to come right out of his skin.

"Porno moans?" Sadie asked Melissa.

Melissa shushed her.

"It's not my fault you muscled your way into my house," Briggs said through clenched teeth.

"You know, it's weird," Kassie said casually. "I didn't used to mind those pathetic noises you made when it was me in your bed. I must have been really desperate—"

There was a loud bang, followed by rain magically coming down right there inside Mystyk Pizza.

Briggs stared at the smoke coming from his fingertips. Horrified, he said, "I think lunch is ruined."

CHAPTER 6

The rain beat down inside Mystyk Pizza, drenching them all as if a hurricane had suddenly arrived. With her hair plastered to her face, Melissa grasped both of Briggs's hands and said, "Look at me!"

Instantly the rain stopped, and she let out a small sigh of relief. But then she glanced around and noted that the damage had already been done. Water dripped down the walls and from the ceiling as if the sprinkler system had been set off.

"Briggs! Look what you did to my outfit!" Kassie cried as she jumped out of her chair and then hurried toward the restroom.

"I don't…" Briggs shook his head. "I haven't lost control like that in years. That's twice in one day."

Melissa stared at Kassie's empty chair. The woman was toxic for Briggs. If they couldn't find a way to get along, it was possible that Keating Hollow would never be the same again.

"You're responsible for this?" a woman dressed in all black asked, her voice stern. She had her black curly hair tied back into a low ponytail and was wearing a pentacle necklace.

Briggs stood to talk to her. "Yes. I can't tell you how sorry I am. I can assure you that it was an accident. I would never do something like this on purpose."

"That doesn't change the fact that you just ruined everyone's lunch or the fact that we won't be able to open again until this mess is cleaned up," she said, barely able to contain her frustration. "Everything needs to be washed down, the linens laundered, and likely the ceiling will need to be replaced. And that's just to start."

Briggs ran a frustrated hand through his wet hair. "I'll pay for all the repairs. Like I said—"

"It's not just the cost, sir. Where are we going to find workers? There's been a shortage for years around here. It will take weeks!" There were tears in the woman's eyes as she gestured around her restaurant. "What are we supposed to do? Close everything down? It's already the offseason. We can't afford to be closed for long."

Melissa wanted so badly to do something—anything—to make the situation better for both Briggs and the owner of Mystyk Pizza, but there wasn't anything she could do. Not right then.

"I'll come after work and get started on the repairs myself," Briggs said. "I used to work in construction while I was in school."

"I'll help," Melissa said automatically. She wasn't sure what skills she could bring to the table, but surely she could do something, even if it was just washing down tables and laundering the linens.

"Me, too," Sadie added. "I'll bring King."

"Me, three," Imogen said.

Then everyone turned to look at Kassie, who'd returned from the restroom. She had mascara smudged under her eyes, and her hair had been wrung out and placed in a sloppy bun on top of her head.

"Not me," Kassie said. "I'll have to get home to rest my voice so I'll be fresh to sing the next morning."

Melissa rolled her eyes and swallowed a snarky remark.

Briggs just glared at Kassie.

"I appreciate that," the owner said. "We'll be here." Then she held her hand out to Briggs. "I'm Bronwyn Woods. I wish we'd met under better circumstances, but I appreciate your willingness to help us get opened back up."

Briggs took her hand and shook it. "Briggs Williams. I really do feel terrible about this, and I promise we'll make sure you're up and running in no time."

"Thank you." She nodded at everyone else and then pulled out her phone and started making calls.

Briggs pulled his wallet out and placed a small stack of bills on the table despite the fact they hadn't eaten anything.

"Now what?" Kassie asked. "I can't go back to the studio without any food in my stomach. I won't have the energy to make it through the afternoon."

"Oh, for the goddess's sake!" Melissa snapped. "There are other places to eat on Main Street. Go find one."

Kassie let out a grunt of irritation and then stalked out of the flooded restaurant.

Melissa slipped her arm through Briggs's and walked with him as they followed Kassie. "You're going to need a change of clothes. Why don't I run you both back to your place? That way the princess won't be complaining all afternoon, and you can grab something to eat."

He nodded. "Yeah, that sounds like a plan."

She waved at her friends, told them she'd see them later back at Mystyk Pizza, and then whistled to get Kassie's attention. She was once again videoing herself on her phone. "If you want to get changed, hustle it up. We're headed back to Briggs's house before you both have to go back to work."

"At least someone has some sense," Kassie muttered.

The three of them walked back to Melissa's SUV with Kassie grumbling all the way. Briggs was silent, and Melissa decided it was best to just let him process. She had no doubt that he was freaked out by what had happened. Who wouldn't be? She didn't have any personal knowledge, considering she didn't have magic, but she certainly knew what it felt like to be out of control.

When they got back to the house, all three of them disappeared to change. Melissa grabbed her overnight bag and changed in the spare bathroom. Five minutes later, she met Briggs in the hallway.

"Are you hungry?" he asked.

"Don't worry about me. I'll make myself something once I get home."

"Home?" he asked. "You mean your home?"

"Well, yeah," Melissa said, feeling slightly disappointed. Somehow, after spending just one night with Briggs, his place had become comfortable. Or maybe it wasn't the house and it was just Briggs. "That was the plan, right?"

He took a deep breath and said, "Yeah, that was the plan. I was supposed to pick you up for our date, and I was kinda hoping you'd end up back here. Especially now that it looks like Kassie will still be here."

"Don't worry about the date. We'll reschedule. As for Kassie, with all the commotion I actually forgot you didn't get a chance to find her some other place to stay." Melissa wrinkled her nose, hating the idea that he might be stuck with her for another night.

"That's right, and I don't know when I'm going to look for one either. We have to get back to the studio, and then I'll be at Mystyk Pizza." He walked into the living room and sank onto his couch, looking like he hadn't slept for days. Though to be fair, he hadn't exactly gotten that much sleep the night before.

"Leave it to me. I'll find her somewhere to stay this afternoon," Melissa said.

"You don't have to do that." Briggs hung his head, looking as if he had the weight of the world on his shoulders.

Melissa went to sit next to him. She placed her hand on his knee and said, "I know I don't have to. But you're having a rough day, and it's obvious you could use a little support. I have time. Let me help."

"You're something else, you know that?" he asked, looking at her with quiet awe.

"I'm just being a friend. You'd do the same for me." There wasn't a doubt in her entire body that what she'd said was true. Briggs was just that kind of guy.

"Thanks," he said.

"Just give me a budget and any parameters, as well as how long you think she'll need the rental, and I'll get it taken care of."

"If you're sure."

Melissa leaned into him, nudging him gently. "I'm sure."

Briggs got out a small notepad and jotted the information down for her. Just as he finished, Kassie appeared from the hallway.

"Did you find something for lunch?" she asked.

"The kitchen is that way." Briggs pointed across the room, clearly done with trying to make peace with the woman.

Kassie stomped away, and Melissa watched her go, wondering what it was like to go through life acting like everyone else was supposed to take care of you. She'd grown up with just her mom and no siblings. She was well accustomed to taking care of herself and wouldn't have wanted it any other way.

Briggs stared after her for a long moment before he turned back to Melissa. "You wouldn't happen to have a calming potion in that bag of yours, would you?"

She glanced at her handbag beside her and then shook her head. "The best I can offer you is an anti-inflammatory."

"Oh, it's not for me. It's for her." He jerked his head toward the kitchen.

Melissa laughed and then said, "If we hurry, we can drop

RISE OF THE WITCH

by Charming Herbals. I'm sure Bree has something that would work."

He glanced at the clock. "If only." He rose and disappeared into the kitchen. A few moments later, he emerged with a granola bar and Kassie in tow. She had a hunk of cheese in one hand and a chunk of sourdough bread in the other.

"I thought dairy was off limits?" Melissa said.

Kassie gave her a flat stare. "I have to eat something. The only other things I could find in Briggs's kitchen were processed meat and fruit leather. That's barely food. Hopefully my tea and honey will be enough to not ruin me for the rest of the day."

"There are other things, but they all require prep and cooking," Briggs said. "Although there are apples and bananas, but Kassie here says those give her gas."

Melissa's lips twitched as she imagined the singer running to the bathroom every two minutes so she wasn't tooting in front of Briggs and Austin.

"I said they weren't great for my digestion!" Kassie let out an exaggerated huff and then stomped out of the house.

Briggs snickered. "Ready?"

"Ready." Melissa quickly grabbed her overnight bag she'd placed by the couch and then walked outside to the SUV. Kassie took her rental car, but warned them she had to turn it in later that afternoon because she couldn't afford to keep it. There wasn't enough room on her credit card.

"I guess I'll be her chauffeur for her stay, too," Briggs had muttered after Kassie took off. Melissa gave him a sympathetic look as they climbed into her vehicle. Once they were back in town and Briggs was exiting the SUV, she told him, "I'll let you know when I find something."

He nodded and then reached out and squeezed her hand. He lingered for just a moment before letting go and disappearing into the studio.

When Melissa got home, she jumped in the shower to take off the chill from getting soaked at lunch. She let the water run over her, luxuriating in the heat. Finally, when she'd started to prune, she climbed out and dressed in her favorite lavender sweatsuit. It was made with the softest material she'd ever encountered and always made her feel extra cozy.

After making a cup of coffee and some toast, she walked into her living room and curled up on her favorite overstuffed arm chair. It was right next to the hearth, and on cold winter days it was the warmest place in the room. As she sipped her coffee, she considered lighting the fire but didn't want to risk abandoning the hot coals when she left to go help Briggs at Mystyk Pizza in a few hours.

Instead, she pulled a throw blanket over her legs and opened her laptop, determined to find somewhere for Kassie Kinny to stay while she was in town. Ten minutes into her search, she broke out the chocolate caramels. Twenty minutes later, she added Irish cream to her coffee.

There wasn't anything in Briggs's budget available within thirty miles of Keating Hollow. Not starting right away anyway. There was a place that was opening up in a week, but it was all the way over in Eureka. She clicked off the short-term rental sites and called both the Keating Hollow Inn and the Book and Stone, the local B and B that was in a lovely refurbished Victorian home just outside of town.

No dice.

In desperation, she called Wanda Danvers, the town's best realtor. After explaining the situation, Wanda said, "I'm sorry, hun. But with Valentine's Day coming up next month, the town is going to be overflowing with visitors. We might be able to hodgepodge multiple places together, but it's gonna cost a premium since there won't be any monthly rates."

"That's what I was afraid of," Melissa said. "Thanks for checking for me."

"I'll keep an ear out. If anything opens up, I'll give you a call," Wanda said.

Melissa ended the call and leaned her head back against the chair. She dreaded telling Briggs the news.

CHAPTER 7

Every muscle in Briggs's body ached. After sitting in the control chair all day at the studio and then ripping out the ceiling drywall at Mystyk Pizza, all he wanted to do was go home, take a shower, and sleep for a week.

"That's all we can do tonight," King said, slapping him on the shoulder.

"Thanks for all the help, man," Briggs said, wiping the sweat from his brow as he watched Melissa and her friends work to clean up the rest of the debris.

"Did you ever imagine that we'd have a circle of people who'd show up for us like this?" King asked Briggs.

Briggs glanced at his friend. "They're here because of you."

King raised both eyebrows. "I'm not the one who made it rain inside."

"You know what I mean." Briggs crossed his arms over

his chest. "If you hadn't found Sadie again, Melissa wouldn't be here, nor would her friend Imogen and her boyfriend Shaun. I just got lucky that I'm friends with King McGrath."

King let out a dismissive snort. "You think I'm the reason that Melissa agreed to be your fake fiancée? Dude, you need a reality check."

Briggs let out a slow breath. "That's not what I meant, and you know it."

"No, I don't know it," King said, sounding slightly annoyed. "Open your eyes, buddy. Melissa is here because she likes *you*, not for any other reason."

"Yeah, okay." Briggs was just finding it hard to believe that so many people had shown up for him. The only person who had ever had his back was King. Not his parents, or his foster parents, and certainly not anyone down in LA. Everyone he'd ever met had always tried to use him to get to King. But Melissa wasn't that type of person. Besides, she was neighbors with King now. Hanging out with Briggs just to be close to King McGrath would be counterproductive.

"Here she comes," King said. "I think I'll go see if Sadie needs help with those garbage bags." He held his fist out, and Briggs bumped it with his own.

King nodded to Melissa as he left, and without slowing down, she nodded back.

When she stopped in front of Briggs, she wore a troubled expression.

"What's wrong?" he asked. Briggs and King had already been hard at work taking down the damaged sheetrock when she'd arrived, and they hadn't had a chance to talk yet.

"I have some bad news," she said, looking apologetic. "I looked everywhere, called the inn, and even called Wanda to see if she knew of anything, but—"

"I'm stuck with Kassie," he said flatly, not really surprised. When he'd moved to Keating Hollow to work with Austin, he'd had a hell of a time finding a rental until he'd closed on his house. He'd stayed at the inn for part of the time and in a short-term rental the rest.

"There's a place in Eureka, but it's not the greatest. I could also cobble together multiple rentals, but they were going to be a lot more than your budget. Even then, there was absolutely nothing during Valentine's weekend. I can try to—"

"No, don't worry about it," Briggs said. "I guess I'll just have to figure out how to get along with her until this album is finished without destroying the entire town of Keating Hollow." Dread coiled in his stomach. What if his magic rippled out of control again? What if someone got hurt... like they had before? He shuddered slightly.

"Do you still want me to come over again tonight?" Melissa asked.

It was on the tip of his tongue to say yes. To ask her to move in with him for the next month or so. But instead, he shook his head. He couldn't do that to her. Melissa had her own life.

"He's lying," King said as he walked by. "He definitely wants you to head over."

Briggs flipped his friend off but didn't contradict his words.

Melissa eyed him intently. "There is no way I believe that you want to spend one moment alone with Kassie."

"That's true. She makes me want to blow things up," he said and then had a vision of doing just that. The ache in his gut intensified. He pressed his hand to his stomach, willing the pain to go away. "But I can't ask you to do that. I'm sure you have a life to get back to."

"You didn't ask. I offered," Melissa said, standing with her hands on her hips and glaring at him as if he'd just insulted her favorite pet.

He couldn't help it. He chuckled.

"That's funny? That I offered? Listen, Briggs, I do have a life to get back to. But here in Keating Hollow, we generally try to look out for each other. If that's too much for you to handle, then I suppose I will just go home. Have a nice night." She turned to walk away, but Briggs reached out and grabbed her arm, stopping her. She paused, looked at his hand on her arm, and then back up at him. "Are you manhandling me?"

"Not yet," he said. "But if you come home with me, I might."

She shook her head in exasperation. "You're a pain in my butt. You know that, right?"

"Yes. But you're going to forgive me and then come save me from the evil pop star. I'll serve you breakfast in bed again."

She stared at him, her eyes narrowed as if she were contemplating his offer. When she finally spoke, she said, "You better."

The ache in his gut eased as he said, "Count on it."

He placed his hand on the small of her back again as he guided her over to where Bronwyn was sitting near the front of the restaurant. The owner was busy working on a list of supplies they needed to continue the work. "Hey, Bronwyn."

She jerked her head up, startled, but then smiled easily at him. "Briggs. Thanks for showing up tonight. Honestly, I didn't really know what to expect, but you and your friends have already made so much progress. If we keep the repairs up at this pace, we might be able to reopen by the weekend."

"I think that should be doable. As long as the paint fumes have dissipated," he said.

"I'm pretty sure we have a witch or two who can help with that," she said with a wink.

Briggs almost said that he could do it, but then he remembered that his out-of-control magic had caused all the damage and didn't want to risk it. "That would be great. We're going to take off unless there's something else you need tonight."

"No. Go home and get some rest. That's where I'm headed." Bronwyn yawned, making her eyes water.

Briggs knew exactly how she felt. "See you tomorrow evening."

Once he and Melissa were outside the restaurant, he turned to her. "Have you eaten?"

"Not much. You?"

He shook his head. "I would suggest a pizza, but…"

She chuckled. "I think we can still get burgers from the brewery if we hurry."

"I'll call them in." Briggs pulled out his phone and ordered three cheeseburgers and fries.

"Three?" Melissa asked.

He shrugged. "One for the princess. I don't know if she'll eat it, but it will be there if she wants it."

"I'm willing to bet she'd rather eat dirt than the grease in that hamburger, but it was nice of you to think of her." Melissa smirked.

He just shrugged because she was probably right. He really didn't know what Kassie would do. Back when they'd had their thing in LA, she'd happily eaten burgers. She'd also eaten waffles and cheesecake and anything else he'd offered. But she hadn't been filming herself every five minutes back then, either.

They thanked Sadie and King and Imogen and Shaun.

"King and I will be back tomorrow night to install the sheetrock, but I don't think there's really anything else to be done until we paint," Briggs said.

"Call me for that," Shaun said. "I'm more than willing to lend a hand."

"Thanks, man." Briggs shook his hand, thanked everyone again, and then walked with Melissa to her car. "I'll go pick up dinner while you pack another overnight bag."

"You have your truck back already?" she asked.

"Yes, it was an electrical panel that shorted out. Thankfully, the parts store had it in stock, and Mitch over at Redwood Auto was able to fix it this afternoon."

"You gotta love small town community," Melissa said.

"The longer I live here, the more I'm convinced it was

the right place to land," he said. "The scenery isn't too bad either."

Her face flushed, and he couldn't help grinning down at her.

"Stop. Go get dinner. I'll see you back at your place." Melissa pushed up on her tiptoes and kissed him on his cheek.

He'd considered shifting just enough that their lips would meet, but he decided he'd save that for later that night when he had time to savor her. As long as he didn't fall asleep first. Now that Melissa had left, that bone-weary exhaustion had started to creep back in.

It was going to be one hell of a long week.

CHAPTER 8

Melissa parked out front of Briggs's sweet yellow house and wondered what she'd find inside. Was she crazy for offering to come over and act as a buffer?

Probably.

But she just couldn't imagine leaving Briggs alone with Kassie. Not after what had happened that afternoon at the pizza place. The way his magic had sparked out of control had rattled her. But at least she'd been able to pull him out of the spell. She'd come to the conclusion that just getting him to focus on something—or someone—else was enough to neutralize his magic. But what if it got away from him again and she wasn't there? Kassie certainly wouldn't be a help then. Not when she was the cause of all his frustration.

Her stomach grumbled as a wave of hunger washed over her. It was enough to finally get her out of her Audi. With her overnight bag in hand, she hurried up the steps onto the porch, and just as she was about to knock, the door swung open.

Briggs gave her a tight smile. "You made it."

"Seems like I'm just in time," she quipped.

"More like ten minutes late." He grabbed her hand and pulled her into the house. "Come on. Your burger is waiting for you."

Melissa let Briggs lead her into the kitchen-dining area, where Kassie was sitting at the table with a deconstructed hamburger in front of her. She'd removed the bun, the cheese, and the onion and was busy cutting the patty with her knife. The fries were nowhere in sight.

"Want something to drink?" Briggs asked Melissa.

"Do you have diet soda?" she asked hopefully.

"Are you kidding? Briggs doesn't have diet anything," Kassie said.

"Sorry," Briggs added. "I'm afraid she's right about that one. I have regular though."

"No, it's too sweet for me. Just water then," Melissa said, musing that she didn't need the caffeine anyway.

Briggs brought them both glasses of ice water and then delivered their plates of burgers and fries.

"This smells delicious," Melissa said right before she picked up the burger and took a big bite. Her mouth was in heaven as she savored the chargrilled goodness.

"Do you have any idea what you're doing to your body when you eat that?" Kassie asked and wrinkled her nose as if she'd just smelled something rank.

"Making it happy?" Melissa chirped as she picked up a fry and stuffed it in her mouth.

"You'll probably wake up with zits all over your face after eating all that grease," Kassie muttered.

"Maybe," Melissa said with a shrug. "But I doubt it, and if I do, well, I sure enjoyed the hell out of myself tonight."

Briggs chuckled softly. "The only thing that would make this better would be a couple of cold beers."

"Too bad they don't let us take them to go," Melissa said.

Kassie got up abruptly and left the room, leaving her half-finished plate on the table.

"Do you think she's coming back?" Melissa asked.

Briggs lifted one shoulder. "Your guess is as good as mine."

They ate in peace after that. Kassie never did come back to the table, so when they were done, Melissa grabbed the plates and stuffed them into the dishwasher while Briggs wiped down the table and counters.

"I feel so domestic," Melissa said as she hung a dish towel on the ring that was mounted by the sink.

"I like having you in my kitchen," Briggs said as he moved to trap her between his body and the counter. "It just feels right."

"You know, that line could sound a little sexist," she said even as she slipped her thumbs into his belt loops and tugged him closer.

"I didn't say you *belonged* in my kitchen. I said it felt right having you here."

"Hmm, okay, I can get on board with that." Melissa stared at his lips, waiting impatiently for him to brush them over hers.

"Good," he breathed. "Because right now, all I can think about is lifting you up onto this counter and—"

"Get a room," Kassie said, breaking the mood entirely.

Briggs took a step back and turned toward the woman. "What do you need, Kassie?"

"Tea," she said. "After all that junk food, I need to soothe my throat."

Junk food? Melissa thought. Sure, a burger and fries weren't the healthiest meal on the planet. But it's not like they had cake for dinner. Not that she was above that. Especially if it involved carrot cake.

"Let's go, Melissa," Briggs said, his voice gruff as he tugged her down the hall to his bedroom. Once they were inside, he leaned against the door and closed his eyes as if he needed a moment to decompress.

Melissa took the hint and left him there while she went to get ready for bed. When she came out of the bathroom, she found him already in bed, his eyes closed and his bare chest rising and falling in a rhythmic pattern. She quietly worked her way across the room, flicked off the lights, and slid in beside him.

Almost instantly, he rolled over and pulled her into his arms, spooning her from behind. "I could get used to this, too," he murmured.

Unexpected tears pricked Melissa's eyes because she didn't need to get used to anything. Nothing had ever felt so right to her.

Briggs pressed a soft kiss to her neck and shortly after she heard the deep, steady breathing of a person who'd fallen asleep.

Melissa covered one of his hands with her own, snuggled in a little closer, and then drifted off to dreamland.

A shout, along with thrashing of the covers, woke Melissa out of a sound sleep. She sat straight up in bed, her heart nearly pounding right out of her chest. "Briggs?"

"Stop!" he cried in his sleep as he thrashed.

"Briggs," Melissa said softly as she placed a light hand on his chest. "It's okay, Briggs. It's okay."

His eyes flew open and he shot straight up in bed. "What happened?"

"You were dreaming," she said carefully.

Briggs stared at her with unseeing eyes. "I was?"

Melissa scooted closer to him and placed her palm against his cheek. "Briggs, look at me. Really look at me."

The glazed look on his face faded as he focused on her.

"Are you with me?" she asked.

"Yeah." He blinked a couple of times. "I'm here."

"Good." Melissa brushed a lock of hair out of his eyes. "Want to tell me what just happened?"

His eyes slammed shut again, and he looked like he'd aged ten years.

"It's okay," Melissa said. "You don't have to talk. We can just sit together, or—"

"It's a reoccurring dream," Briggs said, not looking at her.

When he didn't continue, she asked, "Are you fighting someone in the dream?"

"No." He shook his head slightly. After taking a deep breath, he said, "I'm struggling to control my magic."

Melissa sucked in a sharp breath, but didn't say a word.

He lifted his head and gazed down at her. "When I was young and my magic flared out of control, my father used to try to beat it out of me. One night he went too far and broke my arm. CPS came, and I never saw him again."

"Oh gods," she whispered, squeezing his hand. "I'm so sorry, Briggs."

"I'm not. He was a terrible human. Not that my foster parents were any better. But I did find King there. He's the only family I've ever had."

She wanted to tell him that no kid should ever have to go through any of that, but she was quite certain that he already knew that. Instead, she just wrapped her arms around him and held him close, trying to show him that there were people in the world who cared about him. That *she* cared about him.

"In the dream, I'm using my magic to fight back. I can't control it and…" His voice caught.

"And?" she prompted.

"My magic is choking my father and I can't stop it. It's one of my worst fears, that my magic will flare and someone will get hurt."

It didn't take a genius to realize that the nightmare had been brought on by what had happened in the restaurant that day. She wanted to say something to reassure him, to tell him that he didn't need to worry, but what did she know? Instead, she asked questions. "Has that ever happened before?"

"Have I hurt someone?" he asked.

"Yes." Though she really didn't want to know the answer.

"No, not directly. I have had incidents due to my magic.

Like when I made a mic go flying by accident and it clocked King in the side of the head." He let out a small chuckle at the memory. "He just picked it up and nailed me in the nuts with it. It's fair to say I got the worst end of that exchange."

Her lips curved into a small smile. "Sounds like it. Does stuff like that happen often?"

"No," he said, sounding stronger now. "Not here in Keating Hollow, anyway. It's one of the reasons I moved here. I don't know if it's just that I'm calmer here or if it's the magic that is woven through this town, but I have much greater control over it here. Or at least I did until Kassie started pushing all my buttons."

"Emotions do heighten magic," she said. "Maybe there's something you can do about it. Maybe see a healer or an herbalist to see if there are potions to help you?"

"I've tried that before. The healer said there wasn't anything she could do. The herbalist gave me something that actually made it worse. Apparently it was something to combat my anxiety, but all it did was lower my inhibitions, making it even easier for my magic to run away from me. Now I just try not to use magic very often. Trick my body into thinking that part of me is broken or something."

"So what you're saying is that in order for you to not flood any more restaurants, we need to get rid of Kassie," she said.

"We tried that already," he said glumly.

"Okay, since that won't work, we just need to focus on keeping you away from her outside of the studio. Maybe spend more time with King or your other friends while she's pampering her voice."

"My other friends means you," he said, staring at her lips now. "Are you going to move in while she's here?"

"I hadn't planned on it, but if you need me…"

"I need you," he confirmed. And then his lips were on Melissa's. At first, she held back, not exactly sure they were done talking. But when his hands started to run along the curves of her body and his lips found their way to her neck, she relented and decided that after that nightmare, he needed to lose himself in someone.

And she was more than willing to make the sacrifice.

CHAPTER 9

Briggs walked into the bedroom just as Melissa exited his bathroom, freshly showered and dressed in formfitting black pants and a soft white turtleneck sweater. Her dark curly hair framed her face and he wanted nothing more than to bury his hands in it again.

"You look like you have meetings today," he said as he handed her a mug of coffee.

"I do." She took a sip and pure bliss shone on her face. "This is delicious. I'm gonna have to find out what brand you buy."

He laughed. "It's the beans from Incantation Café."

"Seriously? You'd think I'd have recognized it after all the time I spend there."

"I think your senses are just heightened after last night," he said with a wink.

"I'm sure that's it." She placed the coffee on his dresser,

kissed him softly, and then sat on the edge of the bed to tug on a pair of boots.

Briggs had woken that morning with a pit of unease in his gut. He'd stared at the ceiling, wondering what had come over him when he'd decided to tell Melissa about his childhood. He hadn't told anyone about how he'd ended up in foster care except for King many years ago. It was something he didn't talk about. But the dream had just been so real. He'd felt like he was twelve years old again, right back there in his father's home, trapped and fearful for what each day would bring. When he'd woken, he'd just needed to tell someone… No, he'd needed to tell *her*. To ease his burden and not be judged for it. And she hadn't disappointed him.

But when she'd opened her eyes and smiled at him, the uneasy feelings had faded away. In the light of day, she hadn't suddenly started thinking less of him. She hadn't even mentioned the dream. Instead, she'd climbed on top of him and they'd had another round of lovemaking.

It was why she hadn't gotten her breakfast in bed. Instead, she was getting coffee and a quick breakfast before she took off for work.

"Eggs and avocado toast are ready and waiting," he said.

Melissa beamed at him. "Perfect." She grabbed her coffee and then took his arm as he led her into the kitchen.

As Briggs was handing Melissa her breakfast, Kassie walked in.

"Good morning," she said cheerfully.

Her attitude was such a change of pace that Briggs was stunned silent for a moment. But then he remembered how she'd softened when Imogen had been kind to her and decided that it was worth a shot. If he was going to be stuck with her for weeks, he had to make it work somehow. "Can I get you breakfast, Kassie?" he asked. "There's eggs and avocado toast, or I could make you a smoothie."

Surprise lit on her heart-shaped face. "A smoothie would be perfect. Do you have protein powder?"

"I do," he said and got to work while Kassie made her tea.

Twenty minutes later, Briggs walked Melissa to the door. "Thanks for last night."

She smiled softly, pressed her hand to his chest and said, "No thanks necessary."

They both knew he wasn't talking about their sexcapades. The gratitude was for being a friend when he needed one. "I'll call you later."

She nodded, gave him a kiss, and then left him alone with Kassie Kinny. He let out a tiny sigh and returned to the kitchen to do the dishes.

Once he was done, he was surprised to see that Kassie was already waiting for him by the door. She had her tea in a to-go mug, her laptop bag, and a pleased smile on her face. "Ready?"

"I am." He followed her out, praying that the day was uneventful and he managed to keep his magic to himself.

"How's it going?" King asked as he strolled into the recording studio.

Briggs looked up from his place at the boards and grinned at his friend. "Not bad. We just had lunch."

"Mind if I stay a while?" he asked Austin.

"It's fine," Austin said as he looked at the time on his phone. Then he called, "Kassie, we're ready to go again."

It was just after lunch and so far, the day had been uneventful. All they'd done was lay down track after track on the new song. The one that Austin had finally relented and agreed to turn into a pop song. They'd been trying different vocals and arrangements, while Briggs experimented with the production.

"Just a minute!" she called as she scrolled through her phone for the 200th time that day. Whatever was happening with her social media page, she was ecstatic and kept answering messages even as Austin started to lose his patience.

"What brings you by?" Briggs asked King while they waited.

"Sadie's covering a shift at the brewery, and I didn't have anything else to do, so I figured I'd come bother you. You doing all right?"

"Yeah. Just trying to slog through this song."

"We don't have all day," Austin barked, and Briggs was glad he wasn't the one who had to say it. They had both been getting impatient, but at least Kassie had kept her bad attitude tucked away. Briggs liked to think it was because they'd started out on a good footing that morning.

"Sorry," she said, stuffing the phone in her pocket. "I'm ready." She hurried into the booth and got back to work.

Ten minutes later, Austin tugged his headphones off and

sat heavily in his chair. "Something isn't quite right. Not yet."

Kassie slumped on her stool in the booth, looking both tired and a little frustrated, but she kept her thoughts to herself.

"Do you mind if I try something?" King asked.

Austin glanced at him. "You have an idea? Sure, let's hear it."

King swaggered into the booth, grabbed a pair of headphones, and stood next to Kassie. "Let's take it from the top."

Briggs cued up the music and sat back, waiting to see what King had up his sleeve.

Kassie started to sing, and then King came in with a softer tone echoing her voice. When they got to the chorus, they harmonized, and Briggs just knew that was the magic formula. He met Austin's gaze, and his boss shook his head as he started to smile.

"That's it!" Kassie said. "That's the single." She turned to King and threw her arms around him. "You're a genius."

"I was just trying something out," King said. "You could even do it with just Kassie's voice as a backing track. Layer the lyrics or something."

"No!" Kassie was nearly bouncing out of her chair. "We should do it just like that as a feature."

King pressed his lips together as he contemplated it. "I'd have to talk to my management."

Briggs knew that was a lie. There wasn't anything in his contract that said he couldn't collaborate with another artist. He probably wanted time to consider what it would mean to work with Kassie.

"It really is perfect, King," Austin said. "Give them a call and let me know. I'd love to record this at least as a remix. The label can decide how they want to play it."

King stepped out of the recording studio and Briggs went after him. He found King standing outside, just staring at his phone.

"Gonna make that call?" Briggs asked.

His friend just laughed. "No. And you already knew that."

Briggs leaned against the porch railing. "What made you decide to help Kassie out?"

"I dunno. I just heard the song in my head that way. And you know me; I can't keep my trap shut when I hear the music like that."

"Isn't that the truth." Briggs had known King long before he'd ever gotten a record contract. And as long as he'd known him, he'd always been amazed while watching his friend create music. It was like something came over him and he just lost himself in it. "So, what are you going to do? Sing on her record, or make her find someone else?"

"Would it piss you off if I did it?" King asked, studying him.

"Why would I care?" Briggs frowned at him.

"Because, if I end up on that album, I might have to do appearances with her for promo. She could be around more, I suppose."

Briggs just shrugged. "I think that's something you should be asking Sadie, not me."

King chuckled. "You know what? You're right. I better call her."

"Good luck." Briggs walked back into the studio to find Austin and Kassie playing back the recording with King's backing vocals. Kassie was grinning ear to ear, and even Austin was looking pleased.

When the track finished, Kassie tapped her phone and said, "This is a number one record."

Austin pursed his lips. "Maybe. It does have all the markings of one."

Kassie squealed and bounced around in a circle.

King walked back in and said, "Let's do this."

"Omigods!" Kassie ran and flung herself at him. King barely caught her as she wrapped her legs around him and clung for dear life. "I love you!"

King's eyes widened with panic as he sought out Briggs.

"Better you than me," Briggs said with a smirk.

"Let go of King," Austin said. "Let's get this song finished, and then we'll be done for today."

Relief flooded King's expression once he was free of Kassie's clutches, but Briggs worried he was in for a lot more than he'd bargained for.

As King brushed past Briggs, he muttered, "What have I done?"

All Briggs could do was shake his head.

CHAPTER 10

"That was the perfect day," Kassie said as she walked out of the studio. "I mean it, King. Just perfect. One of those days I used to dream about when I was desperately praying for a contract."

"There will be more days like this," King said as he fell into step beside Briggs.

"Well, we should celebrate this one. What do you say? Dinner at that place with the crab sign in the window?" she asked hopefully.

"Sorry, Kas. I have plans to help Briggs at Mystyk Pizza."

Briggs knew that tone. King was getting irritated, and if Kassie pushed it, he'd shut down completely. "Why don't you go get dinner while we're working, and when we take a break, one of us can run you back to my place."

"It's better than construction work, I guess," she said and then huffed as she took off down the road toward the Cozy Cave.

"One of us?" King asked. "It's going to be you. I already did my good deed for the day."

Briggs's body shook with silent laughter.

"Shut up. You and Sadie warned me about this. But honestly, how can that woman have zero chill?" His dumbfounded expression only made Briggs laugh harder.

"Sorry, man. But you knew what you were getting into," Briggs said. "You can't even deny it."

"I'm an idiot." King sighed.

Briggs snorted. "You said it, not me."

They walked the short distance to Mystyk Pizza and found that Bronwyn had gotten all the supplies they needed.

"Let's do this," Briggs said as he rolled up his sleeves.

King nodded and the two of them got busy redoing the ceiling.

A couple of hours later, Briggs heard Kassie giving a running commentary about how a local in Keating Hollow had lost control of his magic and was now working off his debt to the business owner. He turned and found Kassie videoing the restaurant and then pointing her phone right at him.

"This, my dear followers, is the poor soul who never learned to control his magic. Care to leave him some tips?" She gave Briggs a cheeky smile.

He schooled his features, determined to keep from giving her the reaction she was looking for. Instead, he just turned around and finished installing the next piece of sheetrock.

"Looks like our antihero isn't up for it. Maybe next time.

Until then, kisses!" She ended the video and said, "That was perfect!"

Briggs clenched his teeth, doing everything in his power to ignore her. If he let her get under his skin again, who knew what he'd do this time? Instead, he focused on the image of Melissa's face and the memory of her touch the night before and pushed all thoughts of the media-addicted pop star out of his head.

When Briggs and King finished with the last bit of sheetrock, they told Bronwyn that they'd be back the next night to paint.

"Thank you," Bronwyn said, relief practically wafting off her. "I was so worried, but you guys have really come through. After the painting, all we need to do is a little clean up and we'll be back in business."

Briggs shook her hand, apologized one more time for losing control, and followed King out of the restaurant.

"Want to pick up something to eat?" King asked.

"Yeah. I'm starving." Briggs glanced around Main Street and frowned. "The brewery again?"

"I don't think anything else is still open."

Briggs nodded, and the two of them fell into step together.

"Wait!" Kassie called as she ran to catch up with them.

"She's still here?" King asked softly. "I thought she'd left."

"Not without a ride," Briggs said with a sigh. He was proud of himself for successfully forgetting all about her for the past hour. It had taken some doing, but at least he knew he could do it if he tried.

"Two besties after a long day of work," Kassie was

saying. "And look, with the moon shining down on them, it's like something out of a romance novel, wouldn't you say?" Then she dropped her voice into a conspiratorial tone. "I know there are a bunch of you Bings out there, shipping these two. Add this one to your saved folders, so when they finally come out of the closet, you'll have the proof that you knew all along."

King stopped dead in his tracks while an electric bolt of magic shot up Briggs's spine. They glanced at each other, and Briggs saw the storm raging in King's eyes. He'd had more than his share of crazed fans stalking him. It was the one thing he hated most about fame. They both knew there was some speculation about the nature of their relationship, but that had been in the far corners of the internet where people wrote fan fiction. They'd mostly laughed about it.

But now Kassie was fanning those flames for views. And since she was working with both of them, she'd lend credibility to those baseless rumors.

Kassie snickered to herself and Briggs knew she was done filming. He spun around and glared at her. "Do not post that video."

"Why? It's funny," she said, giving him a mischievous grin.

"Kassie," King warned. "I'm telling you that if you don't delete that video right now, I'm pulling out of the song we recorded today."

Her face went ghost-white, looking sickly under the lamplight.

King's phone pinged with an incoming text. He glanced at it and scowled as he showed it to Briggs.

It was King's manager. The video was already posted.

Briggs reached for Kassie's phone, but when she snatched it away and glared at him, his magic flared out of control again and all they heard was a loud crack, followed by window glass clattering onto the sidewalk.

He stood there, shaking as he took in the scene. He'd shattered the front window of Hollow Books. If that weren't bad enough, magic was still pulsing all over his skin. He closed his eyes, counted to ten, and willed the magic to stop. But when he opened them again, the glow of magic was still there, clinging to him like a bad scent.

"Briggs, I—" Kassie started.

"Don't," King barked. "Not one word from you."

When Briggs's magic crackled again as if he were giving off power surges, King pointed at Kassie. "Get out of here."

"Where am I supposed to go?" she asked, looking downright petulant. "It's not my fault he can't control—"

"Go!" King bellowed. "Before he blows up the entire town."

Kassie took another look at Briggs and then hurried away.

"Briggs?" King said, starting to reach for him.

The magic sparked again, but Briggs barely felt it. He was numb on the inside, watching as magic crawled all over him. He looked up at his best friend and huffed out, "Call Melissa. Get her here, now."

AFTER HER LONG day out on the road, Melissa had gone home to pack some things to take to Briggs's house. When she was done, she curled up in her overstuffed chair by the fireplace with a mug of hot cocoa just as her phone buzzed. She smiled, thinking it was Briggs letting her know he was home. She figured she'd meet him there after he was done at Mystyk Pizza. But when she looked at the screen, she saw Sadie's name instead. "Hey. Are you home? I'm having hot cocoa. I could—"

"It's Briggs," Sadie said, cutting her off. "He needs you."

"What happened?"

"I don't have all the details. All I know is that King said his magic is out of control again and he needs you... like yesterday."

Melissa's pulse kicked up as she jumped to her feet, already headed for the door. As she grabbed her bag and her keys, she asked, "Where are they?"

"Hollow Books on Main Street. I'll meet you at your car."

Melissa rushed out the door. Just as she was climbing into her SUV, Sadie ran out of her house and joined her.

Before Sadie even had her seatbelt buckled, Melissa peeled out of her driveway and sped down the street. "Do you know anything else?"

"No. Only that Kassie pissed them both off and Briggs lost it."

"How this time? Did she try to force him to pay for Botox or something?" Melissa asked, wondering what ridiculous thing Kassie had cooked up this time.

"King didn't say, but I think this might answer some questions." She peered at her phone, upped the volume, and waited as they listened to Kassie imply that King and Briggs were more than just friends.

Melissa's nostrils flared with irritation. "Doesn't that woman know how to go through one day without causing major drama? I swear, she's the absolute worst."

"King is going to hate this," Sadie said. "Not the implication that he might be anything other than straight," she added hastily. "He doesn't care about that kind of thing, but the fan stalking and endless rumors about him have finally died down now that we're together. If the internet takes this and runs with it, who knows what kind of crazy people might come out of the woodwork again."

"It's not just King and Briggs that will have to deal with harassment if people think you two are lying. They'll be calling you a beard and hating on you for pretending to date King. You realize that, right?" Melissa said. The internet was a strange place. It was why Melissa stayed off it most of the time, but she'd gotten to see the darker side of it just a few months before when King had been the victim of internet sleuths stalking his every move. She'd done a deep dive, trying to understand what Sadie was getting herself into. The various corners of the online social media site Reddit had been really eye-opening. She wasn't hopeful that people would be rational about Kassie's engagement-bait video.

"Ugh, you're right," Sadie said. "There are already comments on this video about that." She shut her phone down and shoved it into her pocket. "It's best to not even look."

"Good plan." Melissa slowed slightly when she got to Main Street. When she turned to park in front of the bookstore, her headlights flashed on the damage, making her wince. There was glass everywhere.

But what really stunned her was Briggs. He was sitting on the curb, his entire body glowing with magic.

She slammed the SUV into Park and rushed out of the vehicle toward him. "Briggs?" she asked tentatively as she crouched in front of him. "Give me your hands."

He stood, shaking his head. "I don't want to hurt you."

Melissa frowned at him, rose, and reached for him anyway, but he took a step back.

"Do it, man. You told me to call her," King said. "If you weren't going to let her help, then why—"

"I've had time to think about it!" he shouted, and more sparks flew.

Magic brushed over Melissa's skin, pushing her back a few feet. She let out a small surprised gasp, but she wasn't afraid. His magic hadn't hurt her. She didn't think Briggs had it in himself to hurt anyone. But that didn't mean he wouldn't destroy more property if pushed hard enough.

"See! I just did it again. This magic... I can't..." He shook his head, frustration rolling off him in waves. "I think I might flare out."

Without a word, Melissa walked back to him and wrapped her arms around him.

He stiffened, standing stock still, his magic still casting a glow around him.

"It's okay, Briggs," she whispered into his ear. "You've got this. I know you do." She pulled back, looked him in the eye, and said, "Let it go."

The magic spread, encompassing them both in the soft

glow, and then it just vanished, leaving them there on the darkened sidewalk with just the soft halos from the gaslights lining the streets.

Briggs let out a heavy sigh of relief and then crushed her to him in a tight hug. "Thank you."

"Thank the goddess," Sadie said softly from behind them.

Melissa held onto Briggs, feeling a little shaky. She'd done what was necessary in the moment, but that didn't mean she hadn't been nervous as hell. Melissa had felt like she was flying blind, although knowing she'd been able to pull him out of his magic before had given her confidence. Was Melissa his kryptonite? And if she tried to interfere with anyone else, would the same thing happen, or was there just something special about Briggs? That remained to be seen, but for now she was grateful she'd been able to help.

A car swung into the parking space right next to Melissa's Audi.

Yvette Townsend-Burton jumped out of her vehicle and then stood on the sidewalk, staring at the shattered glass. "What happened?"

Briggs released Melissa but then slipped his hand into hers as he said, "I'm so sorry, Yvette. I lost control of my magic, and it shattered your window. I'll pay for the replacement. And if you need any help cleaning up, I'll do that, too."

Melissa's heart went out to him. That was two businesses in one week that he'd severely damaged. If he kept this up, she was afraid that the business owners were going to ban him from their establishments.

"Do you have it under control now?" Yvette asked, looking more concerned than upset.

"I think so," he said as he squeezed Melissa's hand.

"Good. Magic can be so unpredictable sometimes," she said kindly. "Maybe go see Healer Whipple when you get a chance. She might be able to help."

He nodded, but Melissa didn't think he would take that advice to heart. Not after his last experience with a healer.

"All right. Let's get this cleaned up," Yvette said as she pulled her phone out of her pocket. "Noel? Yeah, I need your help with a shattered window at the bookstore. I'd get Jacob down here, but he's watching the kids. Great, see you in a few." She ended the call. "My sister is an air witch. She'll have this fixed up in no time."

"Can I do anything to help?" Briggs asked.

"Do you have air magic?" she asked.

"I do but..." He sucked in a sharp breath. "Since I'm the one who made this happen, I'm not sure I should be tapping into that again."

Yvette patted him on the shoulder. "When Noel gets here, we'll decide if you're needed."

Melissa stayed by Briggs's side until Noel arrived wearing sweats and a T-shirt arrived. She walked over to Yvette, studied the destruction, and said, "That's a lot of glass to repair."

"Briggs has air magic if you want his help," Yvette told Noel. "But he's a little nervous since his magic caused this."

Noel studied Briggs for a moment. Then she said, "You broke it. You need to help fix it. Come over here."

Briggs glanced at Melissa, his expression panicked.

"I'll be right here beside you," Melissa said, tugging him over to Noel.

"I'm sorry," Briggs said. "I just don't want to cause any more trouble."

"The best way to master magic is to practice control," Noel said, sounding very much like the mom she was. "You just lend me your power, and I'll do all the wielding. That way you can feel me controlling it, understand?"

Briggs visibly relaxed and said, "Yeah, okay. But if things go haywire again, Melissa is here to act as an interceptor."

"You can do that?" Noel asked.

"For Briggs, I can. I'm not sure if it works on other people." She shrugged one shoulder. "I'm not even sure if I'm the one doing it or if I just calm Briggs enough that he can start controlling his magic again."

"That's super interesting," Noel said as she studied her. "You should do some experiments to see. But right now, let's fix this window." She turned to Briggs. "Ready?"

He nodded.

Noel took his hand and said, "Call up your magic."

Briggs closed his eyes, and a moment later, the soft glow of magic covered his hands.

"Perfect." Noel raised her free hand, pointed at the broken glass lying on the ground, and then swirled her finger in the air before she aimed right at the shop where the window used to be.

Magic burst from her finger and spun in a spiral, forming a small tornado. The glass was sucked up into her magical funnel one piece at a time. As the funnel grew larger and larger, the magic covering her and Briggs's hands became brighter and brighter. Sweat started to form on Noel's brow, and Briggs started to shake with the exertion it took to produce that much magic.

Melissa bit down on her bottom lip, praying that Noel knew what she was doing.

"You can do this, Noel!" Yvette called over the wind.

Noel nodded once, looked at Briggs, and then shouted, "Restore!"

The glass flew from the funnel into the window opening, and just like that, the window was back in place without a crack to be found. Though the painted window decoration that had depicted a black bear reading *Winnie-the-Pooh* was now just a hodgepodge of color that looked like a Rorschach ink blot test instead of a drawing.

Yvette clapped and then let out a chuckle. "I guess we're gonna need to clean that and get a new illustration on there."

"At least let me pay for the artwork," Briggs said.

"Nah," Yvette said. "It was due to be changed soon anyway. Don't worry about it." The woman wrapped an arm around Noel's shoulders and said, "Thanks, sis. You're the best."

The two sisters chatted for a minute or two, and then they both got into their cars and left.

King turned to Briggs. "I don't think you should be around Kassie tonight."

"What am I going to do? Kick her out?" he asked, looking troubled. "That's what I *want* to do."

"Yeah, that's what a sane person would do, but we both know that would only make things worse. With the way she documents everything, the next thing you know, you'd be the villain in her social media saga," King said.

"Come home with me," Melissa said, agreeing that the last thing Briggs needed was to be anywhere near Kassie Kinny.

"And just leave her at my house? Alone?" Briggs asked. "I'm not comfortable with that either. With as much trouble as she's been causing, I wouldn't be surprised to get home and find hidden cameras or something."

King let out a grunt of agreement but then said, "I'll go stay there tonight. Tomorrow we'll work on a new arrangement." He turned to Sadie, who silently nodded her agreement.

"There isn't anywhere for her to stay in town," Briggs said. "Melissa already checked."

"Just go home with Melissa and let me work on it," King insisted. When Briggs tried to protest again, King held his hand up. "You've been there for me through all of my drama. I'm going to be there for you now. And I'll be damned if I'm going to let her ruin the good life you have here in Keating Hollow. Of all people, you're one of the most deserving. Understand?"

Briggs hesitated, but as he met King's gaze he nodded. "Okay. Thanks, brother."

Melissa looked at Briggs. "Ready?"

He nodded. "Can you drop me at my truck? It's at the studio."

"Sure." They said their goodbyes to Sadie and King and then got into her Audi. Melissa didn't say anything, she just held his hand as she drove him to his truck.

CHAPTER 11

"So this is your place," Briggs said as he stood just inside Melissa's doorway, feeling like he'd just stepped into a home he'd see in a Hallmark movie. The small two-story house was painted slate blue and had white shutters and wooden planters under the windows that were no doubt filled with flowers every spring and summer. The inside felt like a cozy hug. There were framed pictures of Melissa and a woman he assumed was her mother, along with others that featured Sadie and another woman. Candles were set up on a stone hearth, and what looked like a handmade quilt was draped over the overstuffed cream couch.

It was the type of place that made him think of sharing homemade cookies with a grandmother. Not that he'd ever experienced that himself, but he'd longed for such a scene when he was a kid.

"This is it," she said. "My room is this way." She led him

upstairs to the primary suite that took up the entire floor. She pointed to her second walk-in closet. "There's room in that closet to the left if you need to hang anything up."

They'd stopped at his place on the way home so that he'd have fresh clothes and toiletries.

"I wear jeans and flannels to work. I don't think I'll need any hangers," he said with a soft chuckle as he walked over to the closet and placed his overnight bag in it. The room was spacious with a couple of flower paintings on one wall and a picture of the Keating Hollow River on another. It screamed that it was the oasis of a woman who was content with her life and where she lived.

Melissa shoved her overnight bag that she'd packed earlier in the other closet and then gestured to the sliding glass door. "There's a balcony out there, but it won't get much use until the temperatures warm up a bit."

Briggs moved to stand by the window. He peered out and said, "Nice view of the mountain."

"It is, isn't it? There used to be a bunch of trees blocking it, but once my mom moved to Befana Bay and I claimed this room, I had them taken out. Now I have the forest to the east and the mountain to the north."

"You've lived here your entire life?" he asked, wondering what it would be like to have such deep roots. His own family had moved every few years, and then when he'd been removed due to his father's abuse, he'd been in three different foster homes before finally landing in his fourth, where he'd met King. For a long time, his only home was wherever King was. Now he had his own house in Keating

Hollow. The one that had been invaded by an unwelcome houseguest.

"I have. I've often wondered what it would be like to live in the woods like you do," she said wistfully. "While the view is nice, I still live in a neighborhood with people all around me."

"People? You mean like having Sadie next door?" he asked with a raised eyebrow. "Something tells me that as long as that's true, you're never moving from this house."

She chuckled. "I do like having her right next door. I'm sure you understand since you keep an entire room for King."

He smiled at her. "Yeah. But it's his room. His things. Until he moves them out, it will continue to be his room whenever he wants it."

"I get it." She looked at the bed and then shuffled her feet awkwardly. "Are you hungry? I have leftovers in the fridge."

Suddenly his gut rumbled. When was the last time he'd eaten? Lunch? He and King had been on their way to get takeout when all hell had broken loose.

"That sounds like a resounding yes." Melissa slipped her arm through his and led him out of the room.

Briggs followed her down the stairs and into her bright yellow kitchen with white cabinets and counters. The space had plenty of light, and Briggs wished his own kitchen was so inviting.

"I hope you like tomato basil pasta, cause this chili looks past its prime," she said as she peeked in her plastic containers.

"If it's food, I like it," he said as he moved around her to search her cabinet for a glass.

She glanced at him. "There's soda, juice, or filtered water. Help yourself."

"Want something?" he asked as he pulled the water pitcher out of the fridge.

"Water's good."

He poured them both a glass and then leaned against the counter as she heated up his dinner.

When the microwave beeped, she removed his plate and went to set it on the table. "Dinner's on."

"You're not eating?" he asked as he took a seat.

She sat next to him and shook her head. "I ate something earlier, but I'm happy to sit with you for a while."

He felt a little awkward, having her sitting there just watching him. He wasn't sure why. It wasn't like he never ate in front of other people. Maybe it was just because it was getting late and he was in her house while she waited on him. He wasn't used to anyone except King doing anything for him.

But he had to admit, he liked that Melissa cared enough to pamper him a little.

"Why do you think I can neutralize your magic?" Melissa asked.

Briggs nearly choked on a bite of pasta. He quickly swallowed and then chased the food with his water before he put his fork down and said, "What?"

"You heard me. Every time your magic flares out of control, I seem to be the one who can bring you out of it.

Not even King has been able to help. I'm just asking why you think I'm the one who can."

His heart started to beat wildly against his ribcage. It was the one question he'd been avoiding asking himself. "I honestly don't know. I guess you just calm me down."

She pursed her lips as she narrowed her eyes. "Maybe we should test it. You know, you try some of your magic and I'll... I don't know, see if I can interrupt it?"

Bone-deep wariness rippled through him. "I don't know if that's a good idea. After what happened tonight, I'm thinking I should bury my magic for good."

Melissa stared at him, giving him an exasperated look. "I'm fairly positive that you weren't actually *trying* to use your magic when that window shattered tonight or when you made it rain inside Mystyk Pizza. Those incidents only happened because of Kassie. And she's not here, is she?"

"No, but..." He trailed off, unable to express just how reluctant he was to even think about his magic.

Melissa ran a soft hand down his arm. "Listen, I can't blame you for being gun-shy about calling up your magic after the last few days, but it was fine while you were helping Noel repair the window. I'm just trying to determine what's going on and how I might be able to help you. It's weird for me, too, you know. I don't have any magic of my own and being able to help you control yours is mind blowing to me. If there's more I can do, I'd like to know about it."

She was so earnest, so sincere, that Briggs just couldn't say no. He pressed his lips together in a thin line and then nodded. "Yeah. All right. Let me finish this pasta and then we'll try a few things. Okay?"

Melissa beamed at him, her eyes flashing with triumph.

"Don't act so happy. This could be a gigantic mistake," he said.

"Could be. But I'm willing to bet it won't," she said and then grabbed his fork and took a bite of his pasta. After smacking her lips together, she handed him the fork and then got up to get something out of the fridge. When she returned, she had a slice of cheesecake and two clean forks.

"You're a goddess," he said as he finished off the last of the pasta.

"Pasta and cheesecake. It's the magic formula." She grinned at him and then took a small bite of the decadent treat.

He pushed his plate away and dug into the dessert.

After two more bites, Melissa put her fork down and pushed the plate toward him. "It's all yours."

"Are you sure? Because I'm about to devour the rest of this," he said.

She laughed. "Go for it."

When the last crumbs of cheesecake were gone from the plate, Briggs cleared the table and started to load her dishwasher.

"Hey, you don't have to do that," she said, trying to push him away from the sink. "You're my guest. Not a roommate."

"I'm a friend and you made dinner, so I'm cleaning up," he countered.

"I heated up dinner. It's not the same." She stood with her hands on her hips, glaring at him.

"You put food on the table. It counts in my book." A few moments later, he closed the dishwasher and cleaned out the sink. When he turned back around, she was till glaring at him. He laughed as he wrapped his arm around her shoulders. "Come on. Let's go see what you can do when I make stuff fly off your bookcase."

"Not my books!" she cried.

"Stop me if you can," he said, cackling as he jogged into her living room and then pointed at her bookcase. He called up his magic and held it at his fingertips while he waited to see what she might do.

Melissa stopped right in front of him, her hands up as if she were protecting her books.

He laughed. "What do you think I'm going to do to them?"

"I don't know, but those are my children. So whatever it is, don't make them go flying across the room where they might fall and scuff the covers, or worse, fall open and bend the pages."

"Then you better stop me," he taunted and let his air magic fly.

"No!" She lunged for him, grabbing his hands and instantly neutralizing the magic. But it was too late. He'd already made one of the books fly off the shelf. It fell harmlessly onto the carpet. "Dang it!" she rushed over to it, inspected the book, and then carefully put it back on the shelf. When she turned around, there was fire blazing in her eyes. "I said not to touch the books. And I meant it."

"Okay, okay," he said gently as if he were trying to calm a skittish animal. "Sorry. I didn't know they were that special."

She blew out a breath. "No, I'm sorry. It's just that my mom and I have this thing about collecting special edition books, autographed copies, and rare prints."

He cast his gaze back to the books. "You're saying I just messed with an expensive collector's edition?"

"Expensive?" She shook her head. "Heavens no. The special editions cost a little more than a regular issue, but usually not that much. These are just sentimental, and I try to keep them in pristine condition. As most book lovers do."

"Got it. Leave the books alone." He moved to sit in the armchair by the hearth. "I won't make that mistake again."

Melissa frowned at him as she took a seat at the end of her couch.

"Now what?" Briggs asked, wondering what he did to irritate her this time.

"Nothing." She let out a soft chuckle. "You just sat in my favorite spot."

"Oh, is that right?" He laughed. "Well, in that case…" He sat back and made himself comfortable. "Ready to try this magic thing again?"

"Yes, but stay away from the pictures and the books," she warned.

"Got it. Won't make that mistake again." He winked and then turned to stare at the fireplace. His skin glowed with a faint trace of magic and then suddenly, a fire roared to life in the fireplace. He glanced at Melissa. "Nothing?"

"Nothing. I saw your magic and knew you were focusing

on making a fire, but I wasn't able to intercept anything," she said. "I think I need to be touching you."

"No argument here," he said, unable to keep the self-satisfied smile off his face.

Melissa rolled her eyes at him and moved to sit on the arm of the chair. "Okay, use your magic again."

"So demanding," he said but then focused on the fire again. The moment his magic appeared on his skin, Melissa grabbed his hand and then gasped as the flames burst higher before settling back down to normal. "Whoa, I didn't do that," he said sheepishly.

Melissa was staring at the fire with her mouth open. When she finally met his gaze, she said, "I think I did."

CHAPTER 12

"You controlled the fire?" Briggs asked, his expression astonished. "For real?"

"I think so." Melissa was elated, feeling as if she'd accomplished something she'd wanted her entire life. Her mother was a fire witch, able to manipulate the element. Melissa had always wanted to know what that might feel like, and now she knew. When she'd touched Briggs as he focused his magic, she'd felt alive, powerful, and for once, in control. She'd imagined the flames intensifying, and then right before her very eyes, they'd spiked higher before settling back down to their normal size.

"Let's do it again," he said. "This time I'll manipulate something other than fire."

"I'm ready," she said, perching forward as if she were about to leap off the chair.

Briggs turned and stared at the front door. When his

magic appeared, Melissa grabbed his arm and then imagined the door swinging open, slowly as if someone were creeping in.

The door creaked open.

She let out a whoop of celebration and then called, "Close now!"

The door slammed shut, making her jump up and do a little shimmy as she celebrated.

Briggs cackled. "Great moves."

"I did it! I did it! I grabbed onto your magic and made the door do what I wanted it to do. I'm a genius."

"Maybe, but I think it's more accurate to say that you're a witch."

"No. I can't be," Melissa said automatically.

"Only witches can control magic," he said gently.

"But it's not my magic. It's yours," she said as she pressed a hand to her forehead, trying to make sense of what was happening.

"Mel." Briggs rose from the chair and stood in front of her. "Just because you can't call up inner magic, it doesn't mean you don't have the tools to wield it. You're channeling my magic. It's why you can make me stop when it's out of control. King can't. No one has ever been able to, despite their determination to do so."

Melissa recalled what he'd said about his father. How his dad had tried to beat the magic out of him. She wondered what other atrocious horrors he'd had to live through. It wasn't unusual for kids to not be able to control their magic once they realized they had power. Most had flare-ups and accidental incidents. To have a parent punish a kid for not knowing how to control it was unconscionable. They deserved to have their kid taken away.

"Are you sure that's what's happening? Maybe I'm just interrupting whatever you're trying to do and that's why things went awry," she speculated, but that didn't sound right to her. She'd envisioned what she'd wanted that door to do.

"I guess that's possible," he said. "Maybe we should let you try to control someone else and see if you can manipulate their magic, too. That would answer that question."

Melissa immediately thought of Sadie, but her friend was an empath and could control emotions while singing. That didn't seem like something she could manipulate. But it was late anyway. Too late to call her. "I could ask Amelia. She's a fire witch. Or Hanna at the café. She's a water witch."

"It's worth checking it out, don't you think?" Briggs asked her.

She nodded. "I will. But for now, we know that I can interrupt your magic, which is helpful to neutralize you if Kassie gets under your skin again."

Briggs sat heavily in the chair again, holding his face in his hands. "Gods. I do not want to do any more damage to anything else."

"The only way to be sure of that is to stay as far away from her as possible. At least until you can find a way to control your magic around her," Melissa said.

He let out a bark of humorless laughter. "Hard to do when she's staying in my house."

"King said he'd take care of that," Melissa said, even though she didn't think anything would come of it.

"You know as well as I do that there's nothing available on short notice in this town," Briggs said, sounding resigned to living and working with the woman for the foreseeable future.

"True, but she can't keep living with you," Melissa insisted. "We've got to come up with something else."

He peered at her. "I'm all ears."

She took a deep breath and said, "I think Kassie should move in here while she's in town."

Briggs didn't say anything for a long moment. Then he said, "No."

"No? That's it? You're not even going to think about it?" she asked.

"I'm not unleashing her brand of crazy on you because I can't handle her," he said, determination in his eyes. "Understand?"

"Sure, but that doesn't change the fact that you shouldn't be around her more than is absolutely necessary," Melissa said. "I have a spare room. Why can't she just stay here? I won't even be here for a few days this coming week."

"You won't?" He looked a little panic-stricken at her revelation.

"That's right. I have to go down south to visit some wineries and have client meetings," she said. "I travel a lot. You know that."

"You won't be here if I need you?" he asked.

Melissa shook her head and then climbed right into his lap as she wrapped her arms around him. "Let me do this for you. I know she's a pain in the butt. But I'd feel better if she wasn't antagonizing you at all hours of the day."

"The incidents didn't even happen at home, though," he said.

"True, but don't you think the less time you spend together, the easier it will be for you to just ignore her crap?" Melissa asked. "Right now, it's all day, every day, and all night, too. If you just see her at work, that seems safer. Right?"

A muscle in his jaw twitched. "I hate that you have a point."

Melissa knew she'd won the argument and decided not to push it. Instead, she crawled off him, tugged him up, and wrapped her arms around him, hugging him tightly. When she let go, she said, "We'll wait and see if King comes up with anything. If not, then we'll break the news that the princess has to move here. Deal?"

With a tired sigh, he said, "Deal."

"Good. Now let's go to bed. I have plans for you." She moved toward the stairs, but before she could even make it up the first step, Briggs swept her up in his arms and practically ran to the bedroom as Melissa laughed.

If this was what life was like with Briggs Williams, she was never going to be able to let the man go.

She only prayed that Mr. Noncommitment found a way to come to the same realization. Otherwise, her heart was going to shatter into a million pieces, and she'd only have herself to blame.

When they reached the bedroom, Briggs laid her gently

on the bed, settled himself on top of her, and said, "You're incredible. You know that, right?"

She shook her head.

"Gorgeous, smart, and generous. You're the entire package."

Melissa swallowed hard. Yep, he was going to destroy her. There was no doubt about it. She looked up at him and said, "Kiss me."

"Gladly." His mouth came down and crushed hers, and then for the next few hours, Melissa let herself get lost in Briggs Williams, the man she feared might just be the love of her life.

CHAPTER 13

"Careful, don't sit too close." Briggs's tone was dripping with sarcasm as King took the stool next to him at the brewery. It was lunchtime, and as soon as Austin had dismissed them for their break, he'd hightailed it out of the studio without a word to Kassie. He was done dealing with her beyond what he needed to do for work.

King shook his head, looking disgusted. "You should see the comments on my social media."

"There's a reason why I haven't opened my phone today."

"I didn't either until my manager called to inform me of the gossip spreading all over the internet. I've even been advised to keep my distance from you." He scoffed. "I told him that would only fuel the rumors since we've been best friends for over a decade."

Briggs glanced at King. "If it's better for you not to be seen with me—"

"Stop. I'm not caving to ridiculous internet rumors. And

I'm sure as hell not cutting you out of my life because Kassie-effing-Kinny decided to post baseless gossip on her TikTok just for engagement. I'm not living my life that way, and you know better."

It was true. King and Briggs were brothers, at least in every way that mattered, and they shared a bond that was unbreakable. They'd had each other's backs since they were both seventeen years old. "I do," Briggs said and then asked the question he'd been avoiding. "How'd it go last night with Kassie?"

"As you'd expect. I found her sitting outside the studio, her face buried in her phone. At first the little diva ignored me, but when I told her I'd leave her there, she finally got in the vehicle. Once we got to your place, we both went to our rooms and didn't talk to each other all night. The ride to the studio this morning was much of the same."

"I aspire to be you when I'm forced to interact with people I don't want to deal with," Briggs said and then tried to change the subject. "What are you up to today?"

"Lunch with you, and then I need to sign some paperwork at the studio so that everything is official with the song we recorded yesterday. But I'm going to demand a retraction from Kassie first. I'm just not going to work with someone who lies about me for clickbait."

"Don't blame you one bit. If I were you, I'd pull out altogether, but that's just me," Briggs said, not wanting to have anything to do with the pop star after her antics.

He sighed heavily. "I would, but the label loves the song. They think it's the perfect follow up to the one that Sadie and I just put out. As long as they don't make me do any public appearances with her, I'll let it go. The song is already recorded after all."

Briggs understood. He also knew longevity in his music career was what King craved most. And if the label thought that working with Kassie Kinny was a good move to keep him in the charts, then he would do it. Stability was a driving factor for both of them after their rocky starts into adulthood.

"And then tonight, we paint the ceiling of Mystyk Pizza," King added. "That will pretty much kill the day."

"I bet Sadie will be happy to have you back to herself at night," Briggs said.

"She definitely will be," Sadie said, appearing behind the bar as she tied on an apron. She grinned at them. "Something to drink?"

They each ordered a soda. And then instead of the burger, Briggs went for the chicken wings.

"I'll have the same," King said.

Sadie chuckled. "Of course. I swear, you two could be twins if you looked anything alike." She winked and got to work on pouring their drinks.

Just as Sadie placed their glasses in front of them, a skinny, dark-haired man who smelled like stale cigarettes sat right beside them. He whipped out a camera and took a series of pictures before Clay Garrison, the brewery manager, appeared in front of them.

"Hey, back off!" Clay barked. "This establishment is for patrons only. Leave now, or I'll be forced to call the sheriff's office."

The man stood and shrugged. "Just trying to earn a living, man."

"Earn it somewhere else," Clay said and crossed his arms over his chest as he glared at the man.

"I'm out," the man said. "But just one question, King. Is Briggs Williams your boyfriend? How long have you two been an item? And does Sadie know? Is she your beard? Why don't you two just come out?"

Kings stared straight ahead, refusing to give the man any reaction or comment.

"Briggs, what about you? How does it feel to watch the love of your life act like he's with a woman?" the man asked.

Briggs gritted his teeth and followed King's lead. He knew from past experience that any response would be twisted to fit a narrative. Any narrative. He wouldn't be party to that.

"I said get out!" Clay barked as he came around the counter, his fists clenched.

"I'm going," the man said as he threw a card down on the counter. "Call me if you want to make a statement."

Sadie reappeared, and the man's eyes sparked with opportunity. "Sadie Lewis, how do you feel about being a beard for your supposed boyfriend?"

She stood behind the counter, looking like a deer in the headlights, and Briggs internally groaned when the man snapped her picture. Her face was going to be plastered all over the gossip sites in fifteen minutes or less.

"Sadie," King said softly. "Are you okay?"

His girlfriend met his gaze, blinked, and then nodded.

"Yeah. Sorry. I just wasn't expecting that. I guess I got used to them leaving us alone."

"Maybe it's just a slow week in the gossip landscape," Briggs said, feeling deep frustration that his friend had to endure the public invasion just because his artistry was singing. He knew there was a price for fame, but that didn't mean one should be harassed when they were just living their life.

"They're like sharks with blood in the water," King said, his tone as cold as ice.

They ate their lunch, neither of them talking much. Having the paparazzi show up had sucked all the air out of the room.

When they were done, Briggs threw some bills down on the counter and waited while King gave Sadie a quick kiss goodbye. He glanced at the window, saw the cameraman just staring into the brewery, and scowled. It looked like he wasn't interested in the truth. If he had been, he'd have taken a shot of King kissing Sadie goodbye.

When King joined him, Briggs said, "The paps are still outside."

"I figured. Let's just get to the studio."

They exited the restaurant with their heads down, trying their best to ignore the photographer. But when the man ran up to them and started to play a recording, King stopped dead in his tracks.

It was a snippet of the song that he and Kassie had recorded the day before. Someone—likely Kassie—had leaked it for engagement.

King was practically vibrating with anger.

"Let's go, King," Briggs urged.

His friend hesitated for just a second longer and then strode off down the street with Briggs rushing to keep up with him.

When they got to King's Toyota, he barked, "Get in."

Briggs didn't hesitate even though the studio was only a few blocks away.

King whipped the SUV out of the parking space and sped to the studio. The vehicle jerked to a stop, making the seatbelt dig into Briggs's chest as he lurched forward. And before Briggs could even get out of the vehicle, King had burst into the studio.

As Briggs followed him, he heard him yelling.

"The deal is off!" he bellowed.

Briggs stopped just inside the door as he watched the fireworks go off inside the studio. Austin was nowhere to be found, but Kassie was there with her lips formed into a shocked O.

"I'm not signing off on that song," King added.

"But we had a deal," Kassie said, her face white.

"That deal didn't include spreading speculation about my personal life on the internet, nor did it include leaking the song to the media," King raged. "I'm out. I don't care if it's the biggest hit since the Beatles. I will not have my name connected to you."

"You can't do that!" Kassie shouted right back. "I didn't leak anything. And I didn't say anything about your personal life. I was making fun of people who are delusional about you and Briggs!"

"You heavily implied that Briggs and I are a couple. And now the paparazzi is back in town!"

"Oh, poor King. He has way too much publicity," Kassie said in a pouty voice. "Did it ever occur to you that having people on the internet talk about you makes your music more popular? I did you a favor. You should be thanking me!"

King let out a growl and took a step forward.

"Come at me," Kassie said, making a motion with her hands at her chest as if she were inviting him to fight her. "Show me what you've got, big man!"

"That's enough!" Briggs yelled as he stepped between them. "Kassie, you know what you did. Now back off."

"Oh, now you're going to protect him?" she growled. "Maybe you two really are dating. Just wait until—"

Intense magic burned through Briggs's veins, and suddenly King tackled him as he cried, "No!" The two of them fell through the door and landed on the brick sidewalk in a tangle of limbs.

"What the hell?" Briggs asked as he stared up at the gray sky.

King untangled himself and sat up, holding his elbow close to his body. "Are you hurt?"

"No. But why did you tackle me?" Briggs asked.

"To keep you from blowing up the studio," he said as he climbed to his feet and winced.

Briggs eyed his arm. "You need to see a healer."

"I will if you will," King said. "You have to get that magic under control."

"Thanks for that observation, Captain Obvious," Briggs snarked.

"What in the hell is going on?" Austin asked, appearing out of nowhere.

Kassie stood at the door and started to complain that King was backing out and that they'd had a fight.

King growled and then explained her antics over the past twenty-four hours.

Both of them started yelling again, and Austin put his hands up. "Stop!"

Briggs sat on the sidewalk with his head down as he did his best to keep himself in check. His annoyance at both of them was riding sky high. What he really needed was time away… from all of them.

His wish was granted when Austin said, "Let's take the rest of the day off and regroup tomorrow. "Kassie, keep King's business off your social media pages. And King, let's sleep on this decision. We'll talk more about it tomorrow."

"Fine," Kassie said. Then she looked at Briggs. "I need a ride home."

Briggs didn't answer.

King grabbed his arm and pulled him off to the side. "She can't stay with you. Your magic is out of control."

"I know," Briggs said. "Did you find her a place?"

"The closest place is in Eureka. The place is a dive, but she'll just have to get over it and—"

"I can just see the TikTok videos now," Briggs said with a flat tone. "We can't do that." He rubbed his temple and said, "Melissa offered to let her stay at her place."

"That was generous." King eyed him. "And you said?"

"No, obviously, but I almost blew up the studio, so I don't think I have a choice."

King nodded and walked back over to Kassie. "We've had a change of plans."

CHAPTER 14

Melissa stood at the closed door of her guest room and knocked. "Kassie?"

Silence.

"Are you hungry?"

Melissa heard the creak of the hardwood floors and waited to see if Kassie would answer her. When she didn't, Melissa let out a breath and added, "I'm making dinner. If you're hungry, it'll be ready in about fifteen minutes."

Still no answer.

Well, okay then, Melissa thought. *So much for trying to make her feel welcome.* King had dropped her off a few hours ago, and after Melissa had shown her to the guestroom, she hadn't seen or heard from her since. She padded back into the kitchen where a pot of tomato soup was simmering on the stove. After giving it a stir, she pulled out the sourdough and the gouda she'd been saving just for this occasion.

As she fired up the pan to make her grilled cheese, her

mouth started to water. It had been forever since she'd treated herself to the meal she'd loved as a kid. There was nothing better than a bowl of tomato soup and a grilled cheese sandwich on a cold January day.

Her phone buzzed with a message from Sadie.

You've got to go look at Kassie's latest TikTok.

Melissa let out a groan. *What now?* After she got her cheese sandwich in the frying pan, she turned on the burner and then went to check out Kassie's latest cry for attention.

The video showed Kassie in Melissa's guest room. She was sitting on the floor next to one of her suitcases with clothes spilling out of it, and she had a look of dejection on her pretty face.

"Hello, friends," she said with a sad smile. "Here I am again. It's been a bit of a rough day. My housing fell through. Just completely out of the blue, the friend who'd said I could stay with him decided that lending me his spare bedroom was too much trouble, and he kicked me out with no notice. So now I'm trying to figure out my next moves while I couch surf for a little while. I'm not going to lie. This was a blow to both my creative spirit and my heart. And now my wallet, too, as I try to find a place to stay that I didn't budget for. But I will persevere. You know me. I always pull through. But if you want to help out, go to the link in my bio to buy me a coffee. Every little bit helps." She kissed her fingers and then blew the kisses to her audience before logging off.

The comments were filled with outrage that anyone would do that to her, and most of them said they'd sent her money to get that coffee.

Melissa texted Sadie back. *I swear to the gods, I've never seen such an opportunist. She's shameless.*

That's one way to put it, Sadie texted back. *Good luck with that one.*

I think I'm gonna need it.

Melissa flipped her sandwich and then heard shuffling behind her.

"What's for dinner?" Kassie asked. Her tone was much more hesitant and subdued than it had been the few other times when Melissa had been around her.

"There's tomato soup in the pot," Melissa said. "I'm also making grilled cheese if you want that."

"No cheese, but thank you. I will have some soup," Kassie said.

"The bowls are right there in that cupboard." Melissa pointed to the one to the right of the sink. "Help yourself. There's sparkling water or wine in the fridge. Or water from the tap."

Kassie helped herself without comment and then went to go sit at the table.

Not long after, Melissa placed her grilled cheese and soup on the table and then grabbed a glass of merlot before joining her.

Kassie eyed the wine with a look of longing.

"Want some?" Melissa asked as she raised her glass to her lips.

"I probably shouldn't." Kassie dipped her spoon into her soup and stirred but didn't take a bite.

Melissa was sure she had her reasons, so she didn't try to

convince her. She just said, "Your choice, but if you change your mind, help yourself."

"Thanks." The other woman took a long sip of her water and then dug into her soup. When she was about half done, she looked up and said, "It's been ages since I've had this. It's delicious."

"It's one of my favorites that my mom used to make. The recipe was handed down from my great-grandmother," Melissa said.

"I wonder what that's like?" Kassie mumbled.

Melissa put her spoon down and picked up her grilled cheese. "Your mom didn't cook much?"

Kassie snorted. "Not unless by *cooking* you mean microwave meals. She was always on a diet and only had those diet dinners in the freezer."

"That's rough. So you never learned to cook?"

"I can make a few things. YouTube is perfect for that," she said. "It's fine. I rarely ever think about that. It's just when people talk about normal family things, I always imagine something like a Hallmark scene with mothers who care about more than auditions and fitting into designer sample sizes."

Melissa put her grilled cheese down and picked up her glass of wine. "That's how you grew up? With your mom trying to break into the entertainment industry?"

"Ha! If only. No, she was a stage mom. Always taking me to auditions, singing lessons, dance. Open calls, calls for extras, whatever might help me get credits on my resume that might attract an agent or manager."

There was a bitterness in her tone that Melissa hadn't

expected. Kassie was clearly chasing fame, but Melissa had to wonder if she really wanted it or if Kassie was still just trying to please her mother. "It looks like it worked. You got a record contract."

"Yeah. It did." She stared down at her half-eaten soup. "Now it's all I can do to make sure I don't lose it. If I do…" Kassie bit down on her bottom lip and then gave Melissa a half shrug. "It's stressful. That's all."

"Is that why you're always making those engagement-bait videos?" Melissa asked. "Because you're afraid you'll get dropped from the label if you don't get enough streams of your music?"

Kassie stiffened and then fixed Melissa with a steely look. "It's expected for artists to run successful social media channels."

"King doesn't," Melissa challenged. He had fans in all corners of the internet and yet, all he ever posted about was his music or his scheduled appearances.

"That's because he doesn't have to," she said, sounding angry. "He got lucky having all those internet stalkers and then all that media attention."

"Lucky?" Melissa asked. "I don't think being harassed everywhere he goes means he's lucky. That's no way to live."

"It might be annoying, but it keeps his fans and the general public engaged. People know his name. He doesn't have to post about his day or embellish to get clicks because people are already hungry for information about him. Don't tell me he's not lucky when he doesn't have maxed-out credit cards and a load of debt because he has to take care of not only himself, but his mom, too." She stood suddenly and stalked out of the room.

Melissa stared after her. Kassie might change her tune about how 'lucky' King was if she had any idea that his mother had blackmailed him and cursed Sadie. But it wasn't Melissa's place to tell her anything. That one conversation had shed so much light on why the singer did the things she did. It also sounded like she was supporting her fame-whore of a mother. No wonder her credit cards were maxed out. If Melissa hadn't been so annoyed about how Kassie had treated Briggs she might have even feel a little sorry for the woman.

But Kassie had barged into Briggs's life and made it a living hell ever since she'd arrived. It was hard to have compassion for someone like that.

Regardless, Melissa did feel like she understood the woman a little better. Knowing what made her tick would help while living with her for the next few weeks.

After she finished her dinner and cleaned up the kitchen, Melissa walked through the house, locking doors. Just as she started up the stairs, she heard Kassie's voice and paused.

"No, don't come here," her houseguest said, sounding annoyed. "I'm telling you I have it handled." There was a long pause, and then she continued. "I know what I said, but I'm fine. I just need to get this record made."

Her voice faded out as a door closed, and Melissa assumed she'd gone back into her room.

What was that about? Was Kassie's mom giving her a hard time? Or was it someone else? Melissa shook her head and climbed the stairs to head to her own bedroom. Once she'd completed her nightly routine, she got into bed and texted Briggs.

Are you home yet?

Her phone rang almost instantly. "Hey," she said.

"You haven't murdered Kassie yet, have you?" he asked.

"Yet?" Melissa laughed. "No, I haven't. Not even close."

"Good." He let out a sigh of relief and then yawned. "Sorry. It's been one hell of a long week."

"It has. Did you get the painting finished?"

"We did." He paused and then added, "I wish you were here right now."

"You read my mind," she said, smiling. "But you probably could use a good night's sleep."

"I'd sleep better with you beside me," he countered.

"I bet." Melissa chuckled softly. "Talk to you tomorrow?"

"Tomorrow," he promised.

The line went dead and Melissa snuggled into her bed, missing Briggs's already familiar touch. She let out a groan and hugged a pillow as she rolled over, wondering what she'd been thinking when she'd insisted that Kassie should stay with her.

Oh, that's right. She'd been trying to keep Briggs from destroying anything else. She just hoped he found a way to control his magic soon, otherwise she could be babysitting the budding pop star for weeks. That would mean that any hope of finding herself in his bed again would be nonexistent. And that would be unacceptable.

CHAPTER 15

"Need a ride?" Melissa asked Kassie. She was standing in the kitchen, drinking her coffee, and contemplating fixing breakfast or just finding something at Incantation Café. It was another paperwork day. She had reports to go over before she left town for the next two days.

"Do you mind? That would save me from having to ask Briggs to pick me up," she said. "Something tells me he wouldn't be too happy about that."

There was no doubt about that. After Kassie's over-the-top videos, Briggs would likely be even more annoyed than ever. Besides, as far as Melissa was concerned, they didn't need to be spending any time alone together. Not unless Briggs found a way to control his magic.

"I don't mind. But I'm going out of town tomorrow for a few days, so I won't be here to play chauffeur. There is a bicycle in the garage that you're welcome to use."

"You want me to ride a bike… in January?" she gasped out.

Melissa shrugged. "It's only a couple of miles into town, so I suppose you could walk if you don't want to take the bike. But there's no rain in the forecast, so there's no reason why you couldn't take it if you wanted to."

"Gods," Kassie said, wrinkling her nose. "I can't believe this is my life now."

"You mean the one where you have over five hundred thousand followers, just came off a successful tour, and are recording a new album?"

"No. The one where I'm stuck in Keating Hollow, living with my ex's fiancée and riding a bike to work," she spat out.

Fiancée. Melissa had almost forgotten about that lie.

"What I don't understand is why you two don't live together already. Isn't that what engaged people do?" Kassie asked, studying Melissa.

"Some do, I suppose. It takes all kinds, right?"

"Looks like it." Kassie poured her tea into one of Melissa's to-go mugs and said, "I'm ready."

"Great." Melissa grabbed her laptop and her red faux fur coat and led the way outside.

Kassie ran to catch up with her, and when she jumped into the Audi, her teeth were chattering from the cold. "No one told me I'd have to endure Siberian temperatures."

"It's forty-five degrees out. Hardly Siberian temps," Melissa said.

"Well, it's not seventy like it is in LA right now," Kassie grumbled.

Melissa let out a disbelieving laugh. "Is there anything you don't complain about?"

"This week? No." Her phone rang. She looked at the screen, frowned, and then answered it. "I told you, I'm fine. I'm on my way to work now."

Melissa could hear someone talking on the other end of the line but couldn't make out the words.

"No. Do. Not. Come. Here." Then she ended the call.

"Was that your mother?" Melissa asked as she turned onto Main Street.

"My mom? No." Kassie gave her a crazy look. "Why would you think that?"

"I dunno. Last night you said she was a pretty aggressive stage mom. I just thought maybe she wanted to see what you were up to."

"Oh. That. Well, she doesn't really have the means to follow me around the state, otherwise she *would* be here," Kassie said bitterly. "It was one of the perks of recording here. That was a… um, friend. Well, more like a fan who wants to come and save me from my living situation." She smirked. "People take my TikTok videos too literally."

"Maybe if you were more honest, they wouldn't get so riled up," Melissa offered.

"If they didn't get riled up, they wouldn't be super fans," Kassie said.

"I suppose they wouldn't." Melissa pulled into a spot right beside Briggs's truck.

Kassie jumped out and hurried into the studio.

Briggs popped his head out the door, and when he

spotted her still idling in the space, he hurried out and stopped at her door. After she lowered the window, he said, "Hey, gorgeous."

"Hey yourself. Did you sleep well?"

"No. I kept reaching for a gorgeous brunette, only she wasn't there. Made my bed feel awfully empty," he said, staring at her lips.

"I know the feeling," she said breathlessly.

"You were also missing a gorgeous brunette?"

She gave him a cheeky grin and ran her hand through his dark hair. "Yeah. I was."

He bent down, cupped both of her cheeks, and kissed her so thoroughly that even her toes tingled. When he stepped back, she was breathless.

"Can I take you to dinner tonight?" he asked.

"And leave Kassie on her own?"

He nodded. "She'll survive."

"I suppose she will. Pick me up at six?"

"I'll be there." He winked and strode back into the studio.

Melissa was just about to raise her window when she spotted King's Toyota pulling in beside her.

"Hey," she called once he was on the sidewalk.

King jerked his head up, spotted her, and immediately made his way to the driver's side of her Audi.

She said, "Are you recording again?"

"No. I'm just here to keep an eye on Briggs. And to get Kassie to pull that damned video."

Melissa knew he was referring to the one that speculated about their sexuality. "Do you think she will?"

"If she wants our single to come out, she will. If not, I'll bury it. If she makes a fuss, I'll sue for libel." His expression was stoney. "The harassment is getting worse. Last night, random people started texting Sadie, and she had to turn her phone off. I think she's getting a new number today, so if you have trouble reaching her, just wait until she contacts you."

A pit of unease settled in the middle of Melissa's gut. "Sadie's getting unsolicited texts?"

"You could say that. She's gotten questions asking how much she's been paid as a beard, others that are AI images of me and Briggs acting like a couple, and still others that are soliciting her for when she breaks up with me."

"That's awful." Bile rose to the back of Melissa's throat. "Maybe I should go over to her house."

"She's already left, but if you hurry, you might catch her at Incantation Café," he said.

"Then I better get moving. Keep an eye on our boy," she added and then raised the window and drove the three blocks to the café.

"Sadie!" Melissa called, spotting her friend coming out with a drink carrier in her hand.

"Mel?" Sadie peered at her and then smiled. "Is it a café workday?"

"It was going to be, but now that depends on you. What are you up to?"

"I'm taking this coffee to Imogen's to check out her new party space. Want to come?"

Melissa gripped her steering wheel, knowing that she should go inside and get to work, but she really needed to talk to her friends about everything she'd learned about her ability to disrupt magic and her insane insistence to house Kassie Kinny. "Let me get my coffee and pumpkin bread, and then I'll be ready."

Fifteen minutes later, Sadie and Melissa walked up the stairs onto Imogen's porch. It had been freshly painted white with slate blue shutters and trim, and there were inviting wicker chairs where Melissa could imagine her friend having her afternoon coffee every day.

"Sadie!" Imogen called as she opened the door. Then she spotted Melissa. "Oh, excellent. You came, too. Perfect. Come in."

The three of them walked into the cozy house, and it was so warm that Melissa had to instantly ditch her red coat. She placed her coffee and pumpkin loaf on the nearby table and glanced around. "Imogen, this is really charming."

"Thanks," the other woman said. "I've been working on it."

Working on it was an understatement. The place looked like something right out of *Architectural Digest*. The wood floors had been sanded and refinished, making the wood gleam. The entire inside had been painted, and the furniture looked like something right out of a Pottery Barn catalog. But the kitchen was the real beauty. She'd refinished the cabinets to a seafoam green and added new white marble countertops and a white farmhouse sink. It truly was lovely.

"Will you come decorate my place if I ever get around to updating it?" Melissa asked.

"Your place is already perfect," Imogen said. "But if you want a change, of course I'll help."

Melissa smiled and said, "It really is perfect, isn't it?"

"Shut it," Sadie teased. "If anyone needs a home makeover, it's me. You girls don't know what happens to your place when a man moves in. I now have a television screen that covers my entire wall and the surround sound speakers to go with it. I feel like I'm living in a movie theater, only there's no stale popcorn or thirty-dollar drinks to be had."

They all laughed. Then Imogen gave them a tour of her place. "It's small, but I think it's going to be perfect."

"I don't think there's any question. It's already perfect," Melissa said, smiling at her friend. "I'm just so happy for you."

Imogen moved in for a hug. "Thank you. You don't know how much this means to me after everything I've been through."

"We have an idea," Sadie said, squeezing her hands and staring pointedly at her.

About a year before Imogen had moved to Keating Hollow, she'd been possessed by a ghost. An evil one. Imogen had almost lost everything, including her sister, due to the ghost's antics. Eventually, her sister Harlow had broken the curse and Imogen had gotten her life back. Now she was dating, running her own business, and had even purchased the property that included her small house and ginormous barn.

"Okay, enough about me," Imogen said as she invited them to sit at her small table. "What is going on with the pair of you? I heard the rumors about King and Briggs. Has that turned into a thing?"

"Yes," Melissa said at the same time Sadie said, "No, not really. That doesn't mean he's not pissed as hell, though."

Melissa and Sadie looked at each other and then started to laugh.

"It's only a thing with Briggs because he keeps getting irritated with her, and it makes his magic flare out of control," Melissa said.

"And King is angry because we're both being harassed," Sadie explained. "He's been asked by every publication out there how long he and Briggs have been an item. I mean, what do they expect him to do, accidentally spill some tea for their gossip rags? Instead, we just ignore it all."

"That's the best plan," Imogen agreed and then turned her attention to Melissa. "Tell me about this magic thing. Has it happened again?"

Melissa nodded and told her about the window shattering at Hollow Books. "He literally can't control it. I've had to intervene a few times to help avoid disaster."

"How?" Imogen asked, her brow furrowed. "What did you do? Throw your body between this woman and one of his spells?"

"Now that would be exciting," Sadie said with a snort.

"No. Not like that." Melissa explained how all she had to do was touch Briggs and it interrupted his magic. "Like I did at the pizza place. But I also learned that I could *control* his magic if I concentrate."

"You can?" Imogen's eyes were wide with wonder. "Have you always been able to do that?"

"No... Well, I don't know, I guess," she said. "I always

thought I didn't have any power, but it looks like I can wield other people's magic, which is quite the gift."

"Or weapon, depending on how you look at it," Imogen said.

"Definitely. I just didn't want to voice that because I'm not interested in weaponizing any magic. I just want to make sure that Briggs and all of my friends are protected and safe."

Imogen moved closer to Melissa. "We need someone who has magic so we can test the theory and see if you can control it."

"I don't—" Melissa started, but she was cut off when the front door slammed and in walked Amelia Holiday-Riley in her Keating Hollow Fire Department uniform.

She glanced around. "I'm here to inspect the barn for the activities permit."

"Right," Imogen said. "Can you believe that I forgot all about that?"

"It's not sexy like wall color or light fixtures. Most people just don't care," Amelia said.

"Come on," Imogen said, taking her arm. "Let's go do that, and then we're kidnapping you so you can get caught up on everything that's been going on."

Sadie and Melissa sat at the counter, sipping their coffees as they waited for Imogen and Amelia to return. When they did, the two were laughing and in good spirits.

"Good news, Melissa," Imogen said. "Amelia has offered to be your guinea pig."

"What?"

"You heard me. She's a fire witch, so if you really can

control other people's magic, this will be an easy one to test."

Melissa looked at Amelia with trepidation. "Are you sure you want to do this?"

"Oh, yeah," she said excitedly. "I've never met someone who can take over another person's magic. I'd love to be your test subject."

"If you're sure…"

"I'm sure. Let's do this outside though… just in case," Amelia said.

Melissa followed her toward a soggy place behind the barn.

Amelia abruptly turned and said, "Try your magic now."

Caught off guard, Melissa had to center herself first, but then reached out with her mind to see if she could sense Amelia. She did, almost instantly.

"Good. Now see if you can stop this." Amelia tossed a bolt of fire toward the soggy pond.

Melissa struggled to focus at first, but then just as she was about to give up, she felt the tingling thread of magic tethered to her friend's fingertips. She met Amelia's gaze, nodded once, and then made the bolt of fire dance around the makeshift firepit.

"Oh my gosh," Sadie said with reverence as she stared wide-eyed at Melissa. "It's official. You are a witch!"

"No, I—"

"You are," Amelia confirmed. "Only someone who is very powerful could do something like that."

"Well, I used *your* magic," Melissa reminded her. "That's the reason why it's so strong."

"Do it again," Amelia ordered.

Melissa did as she was told and sent the fire straight up in the air, managing to avoid burning anyone or anything.

Everyone stared at her, their mouths gaping open. Then they laughed, and Sadie said, "I sure am glad you're on my side."

"Always," Melissa said. "Now, let's go look at this barn."

CHAPTER 16

Briggs sat at his computer, palms sweaty as he clicked the link that had been provided for him. That morning when he'd woken up, he'd lain in bed, hating that Melissa wasn't there. Or more accurately, that she wasn't there because he couldn't keep his emotions in check.

Every time his magic flared out of control, fear settled into the crevices of his heart. What if he was never able to control it? Would he eventually have to cut himself off from everyone he loved just in case he got upset about something? Images of his father breaking his arm flashed in his mind and made his stomach roll.

There were two choices; he could continue to live with the consequences or try to do something about it. Seeking a traditional healer hadn't worked. Neither had self-medicating with potions.

His last resort was to try therapy. He'd contacted Healer

Whipple, the well-respected healer in town, and had gotten a referral for a therapist who specialized in dealing with magic disorders.

Much to his surprise, when he'd inquired about getting an appointment, Dr. Blackwood had messaged back that he had an opening that afternoon. Briggs had taken it on the spot. Thankfully, Austin hadn't had a problem with him leaving early that day. So there he was, getting ready to spill his guts to a stranger in hopes they had some sort of ability to help him control his emotions.

The voice in his head told him it was all woo-woo BS, but nothing else had helped. What did he have to lose?

Briggs clicked the link and the video chat came up on his screen. Dr. Blackwood was already in the video, a welcoming expression on his face. The older man had salt and pepper hair, kind eyes, and deep laugh lines. His appearance immediately put Briggs at ease.

"Good afternoon, Mr. Williams," Dr. Blackwood said. "I see from my notes that you're having some trouble controlling your magic."

"Yes, that's true," Briggs said. "There is a person who has recently come into my life that really gets under my skin, and every time I get angry, my magic manifests in unpredictable and destructive ways." He went on to explain the rain and the window incidents and how Melissa had been the only one who seemed to be able to help him break out of the cycle.

"Your girlfriend calms you down. That's a sign of trust. You must have a pretty good relationship," the doctor said as he made a few notes.

"Well, she's not exactly my girlfriend. More like a friend," Briggs hedged. Outside of their pretend engagement and physical intimacy, he and Melissa hadn't had a conversation about any sort of commitment. Sure, they had plans for later that evening, but it was their official first date.

"Do you have a romantic relationship with this woman?"

"Yes, but we aren't committed," Briggs clarified.

The doctor looked up at him curiously. "Why not?"

Briggs let out a bark of laughter and explained how he'd begged her to pretend to be his fiancée, and that up until this week, they'd just had a flirtatious and friendly relationship. "I've never been the commitment type."

"What about her?" he asked. "Does she want more than something casual?"

"Yeah. She says she's looking for Mr. Right, not Mr. Right Now." Briggs frowned at him. "What does this have to do with me not being able to control my magic?"

"I'm not sure yet." The doctor smiled easily at him. "I'm just trying to get to know you a little bit and understand your existing relationships. Let me make sure I'm understanding this correctly. You are in a physical relationship with Melissa, but she isn't your girlfriend. You'd classify her as a friend. Right?"

"Yes," Briggs agreed.

"And she appears to be the person you trust over everyone else?"

"No." Briggs shook his head. "That distinction goes to my brother, King. He's been my only family since I was seventeen years old." Briggs took a few moments to fill him in on their shared history in the foster home and how they were always there for each other through whatever life threw at them.

"Tell me about that," Dr. Blackwood said. "What have you two been through besides navigating the foster system?"

"Isn't that enough?" Briggs asked, his voice cold.

"I wouldn't use that expression, but I am aware of the trauma that is caused by losing one's family and having to adjust to a foster situation that isn't ideal. It appears to me that you both leaned on each other during that time. I'm quite certain you two share a bond that will endure for the rest of your lives. I just want to know how your relationship has evolved since then."

Briggs didn't understand why the doctor wanted to focus on the two relationships that meant the most to Briggs when clearly his trauma was with his parents and his foster homes. But he found it easy to talk about his best friend, so he dove in. "After King and I left the foster home, we worked all kinds of jobs to stay afloat. King was always trying to break into the music business, which took a lot of his time, and he didn't get paid very well in the beginning. So I worked two and three jobs, making sure we had our rent paid. He pitched in whatever he had, but in those early days, it was a struggle.

"Then as King started getting more and more gigs, the finances evened out, and King made a point of paying me back. That was when I started saving for my house here in Keating Hollow." Briggs swallowed, trying to hold back his emotion. "King even offered to help with the downpayment on my house, but I refused. I wanted it to be something I'd accomplished just for me if that makes sense. King's star had started to rise. He was out on the road a lot, and when he wasn't, he was getting more and more famous."

"And how did you deal with that? Your best friend was being pulled in many directions. Did you feel left behind?"

"No. Not at all." Briggs shook his head. "King always made a point of including me. And then as his fame grew, I started acting as sort of a buffer between him and his fans. Kind of like a bodyguard if you will." Briggs explained all the insane fan behavior King had endured and how Briggs had been the one to shield him from a lot of it.

"You became his protector," the doctor clarified. "And you gave him his own room in your house."

"Yeah. Exactly. But he's family, so it's not like any of that was a sacrifice," Briggs said, feeling a little defensive.

"Is that how you feel? Like you sacrificed part of your growth for your friend?" Dr. Blackwood asked.

"No. Not at all. Didn't I just say it wasn't a sacrifice?"

"You did. I just found it interesting that you used that word and wanted to clarify." The doctor put his pen down and peered into the screen. "It sounds like your relationship with King is a little co-dependent, but that's understandable considering your shared history."

"We share trauma. That's not shocking."

"No, it isn't. But it might also explain why King isn't the person who can help you control your magic when it flares up. That trauma response is always in the background whether you know it or not."

Briggs shrugged. "Okay. But I don't need to know why King can't help me. I need to know how I can help myself."

"We're getting there. This is all part of it. Are you ready to talk about your parents?"

"No," Briggs said. "I'm never ready to talk about them."

The doctor nodded. "We don't have to do that today, but it would be helpful for me to understand your background."

Briggs sucked in a sharp breath. "I'll just tell you that even as a kid I had trouble controlling my magic. As most kids do. But my father wouldn't tolerate anything less than perfection, and he tried to beat my disobedience out of me. At age twelve, he broke my arm, and that was the last time I saw him or my mother." He glanced away, unable to meet the therapist's eyes.

"I see."

Briggs heard him scribbling notes but still didn't raise his gaze.

"Do you want to tell me how you feel about your parents now?" Dr. Blackwood asked.

"I'm pretty sure you can guess."

"I could, but that wouldn't make me a very good therapist," he said kindly. "How about you just tell me how you feel when you think of them?"

Briggs closed his eyes. "Resentful. Betrayed. Abandoned. Unlovable."

"That's enough," Dr. Blackwood said softly. "Are you okay to continue, or do you need a break?"

"I'm fine," Briggs insisted as his eyes flew open. "I just want some tools to help me control this magic so that I don't hurt anyone."

"Okay. That's good. Now, tell me about this woman who

is back in your life. The one causing your magic to flare. What does she do that gets under your skin?"

"I don't think this appointment is long enough to explain all that," Briggs joked. But then he launched into how they'd had a fling, he'd ended it, but she never got the message. Then how she'd shown up and manipulated her way into staying with him, and now she was using him and King to further her engagement online.

The doctor nodded as he took it all in.

When Briggs finally finished, he added, "I can't stand the manipulation. It makes me feel trapped."

The doctor smiled at him. "There it is. The underlying reason why she gets to you so badly."

"That's hardly a revelation," Briggs said flatly.

"But do you know why that manipulation triggers your magic?"

"No. I'm not reaching for it, and I rarely use my magic anyway. I don't know why it happens, only that I don't want it to," Briggs said.

"I'm going to guess that this Kassie person tries to manipulate you in the same ways that your father did," the doctor said. "The way she doesn't listen to you or respect your wishes touches that wound left by your father. She's not physically violent, but her words are carefully crafted to get what she wants from you, and when she doesn't, she finds a way to punish you. Whether that's with a biting remark, or using you for her personal gain, or deliberately pushing your buttons to get a reaction, it all goes back to the same thing. While your father was trying to beat your magic into submission, he instead conditioned you to lash out with it. Now you're doing the same with Kassie."

Briggs sat with that for a long moment. Then he nodded. "I suppose if I'd had a little bit of distance, I could have seen that myself."

"One rarely does, Briggs. Not when childhood trauma is involved. Now about those tools. Are you ready for some suggestions?"

"Please." A sense of relief started to sweep through Briggs. He didn't know if the suggestions would work for him, but just talking to the therapist had helped validate some of his feelings. It made him feel like he wasn't crazy after all.

"First, I want you to think of a place where you feel safe. Your comfort zone if you will. That can be a physical place. Or it can be a person. Or even an object if it calms your soul."

"A safe place. All right."

"Close your eyes and wait for it to come to you, and when it does, tuck it away in the corners of your mind. Make it vivid enough that when you need it, it's easy to call up."

Briggs did as he was told and thought that an image of his pretty yellow house would appear. It was the one thing that was truly his. Something that he'd earned. And he loved it. But instead, Melissa's kind eyes and sweet smile were there, gazing at him. His eyes flew open, and he blinked rapidly.

"Your safe place was a surprise to you." The doctor's words were a statement, not a question.

"Yes," Briggs said.

"I'm going to guess your safe place is the person you trust the most in this world. And it's not King."

"King should be my safe place," Briggs said, frowning. How could Melissa be the person he trusted most when he'd only known her for a short time?

"Oftentimes, one's safe place is with the person who has never let them down or who has an energy that is grounding," Blackwood said.

"In this case, it's both," Briggs admitted.

"Okay. That's good," the doctor said with a nod. "Now, this is what I want you to do when you start to get worked up to the point that you feel like you're going to lose control; I want you to envision your safe place. Latch onto the emotions you feel when you're in their presence and let go of the frustration that's wound you up so tightly that you fear you'll lose control."

"So you just want me to think of Melissa?" Briggs asked, feeling like that was too easy.

"No, Briggs. I want you to remember how you *feel* when you're with her," he emphasized. "When you have your guard down and don't feel the need to protect yourself."

That lightbulb moment went off in Briggs's head. Of course. All the uncontrollable magic. Why he couldn't stop even when he wanted to. His father's fists had trained him to protect himself at all costs.

Dr. Blackwood smiled at the expression on Briggs's face. "Well, I think we've had a very productive chat today. Should we set up another appointment for next week to see how things progress?" he asked.

"Yeah, okay," Briggs said.

"I'll email you the calendar so you can pick a time and date. Have a good evening, Briggs."

The video of the doctor disappeared from his laptop screen, and Briggs sat at his desk, feeling somewhat shellshocked. It had only taken one appointment to get right to the heart of things. He was under no illusion that he'd be fixed overnight, but he did have hope that he was finally on the right track.

CHAPTER 17

Melissa eyed herself in her full-length mirror and wondered if she was too dressed up. She'd opted for a black dress that had a hint of shimmer, black boots, and her red faux fur coat. The bodice of the dress showed just the right amount of cleavage so that it was sexy, but not too revealing. But if Briggs decided to take her to a movie or somewhere like mini-golf over on the coast, she'd definitely be overdressed.

The only question was, did it matter?

No. If that's what they ended up doing, she'd just pretend they were going somewhere fancier later. With a self-satisfied smile, she dabbed on her favorite red lipstick and went downstairs to wait for her date.

"Hot damn. Where are you headed, the Hustler Club?" Kassie asked.

Melissa ignored the slight. She had eyes and knew she

didn't look like a stripper or even a high-class call girl. "I have a date."

"And you trust me here all alone?" Kassie asked.

"What are you going to do, bug the entire house with cameras? Good luck with that. The most exciting thing you'd see me doing is drinking wine while I read by the fireplace. Besides, I'm going out of town tomorrow for a few days, so you'll have the place to yourself anyway."

"Really?" The singer looked a little shocked.

"Really. I have a job to do. Just don't burn the place down, and we'll be good."

Kassie gave her a small smile. "I think I can handle that."

There was a knock on the door, and Kassie ran to open it before Melissa could get to it.

"Briggs," she said, placing her hand on his chest. "I just wanted to apologize about that video. King and I spoke and—"

"I know you took it down," he said as he physically removed her hand from his body.

Melissa was glad he did it so that she didn't have to.

"Right, but I wanted to tell you that I was just joking because of the dumb rumors on the internet and—"

"It doesn't matter." Briggs stood on the doorstep and stared at the musician with mild disdain before he looked past her. His expression shifted instantly as a sexy half smile claimed his lips. "You look incredible."

Melissa felt her cheeks flush with pleasure. "I hope you're taking me somewhere worthy of this dress. If not, I might have to just take it off."

"I'll help you with that, but later. For now, keep it on. I want to show you off a little."

"Oh gods," Kassie said dramatically. "You two are gross, you know that?"

Neither Briggs nor Melissa acknowledged her comment.

Melissa grabbed her red bag and swept past Kassie. Briggs leaned in to kiss her on the cheek and then led her outside onto the porch.

As they were making their way to his truck, Kassie called, "Be safe! Don't forget the condoms!"

Briggs smirked and whispered, "Don't worry. I didn't."

Melissa chuckled. "If you think I'm getting busy in the back of your truck, you're not as bright as I thought you were."

"What if I have a sleeping bag back there?" he teased. "A night under the stars sounds just about perfect if you ask me."

"If it wasn't forty degrees out, maybe," she countered.

"Don't worry. I'll keep you warm," he said with an exaggerated wink.

Melissa threw her head back and laughed. "You're ridiculous."

"But I made you laugh, right?"

"True."

Briggs opened the truck door for her and made sure she was safely inside before gently closing it.

"Such a gentleman," she said once he was in the truck.

"It's our first date. I'm pulling out all the stops." As he steered the truck toward downtown, he reached over and took her hand in his and brushed his thumb over the back of her hand. "Did you have a good day?"

"I did," she said, feeling a warmth in her chest. "I spent some time with Imogen and Sadie over at Imogen's new place. While we were there, Amelia Holiday-Riley stopped by and helped me figure out that it's not just your magic I can control. I can wield hers, too. So while I may not have magic of my own, it looks like I can harness other people's magic."

"Wow, really? That's pretty rare, isn't it?"

"I don't know," she said with a nervous laugh. "I suppose."

Briggs shook his head as he let out a soft chuckle. "We're quite the pair. Here I am, an elemental witch, with more magic than I know what to do with, and you… Well, you don't have any of your own but seem to wield it like a pro."

That sounded like the perfect match to Melissa, but she kept that thought to herself. "Well, it's not like I intend on using this newly discovered power. What would I even do with it? Just walk up to someone while they're casting a spell or charm and just take over? Seems pretty invasive if you ask me."

Briggs brought her hand to his lips and kissed her knuckles. "I can't imagine you'd do such a thing, but I, for one, am grateful you've been there to help me."

"Me, too," she said softly, suddenly feeling shy. "Anyway, enough about that. After my visit, I went home and got caught up on work, so I'm ready for my meetings over the next few days. Now tell me about your day. Sadie said it looks like King and Kassie came to some sort of agreement."

"They did. Kassie was pretty freaked out about King backing out of the song, so she apologized profusely and then was on her best behavior for the rest of the morning. Honestly, she was more like the Kassie I knew back in LA instead of this new caustic, fame-hungry version she brought to Keating Hollow."

"That's good, right?" Melissa asked. But even as the words came out of her mouth, she felt a little nauseated by the thought of Kassie and Briggs when they were back in LA. They'd been a thing then. It wasn't something she liked to think about.

"Yeah. It is. King is still irritated about it all, but at least he's not threatening lawsuits anymore. And hopefully Kassie will decide that she can catch more flies with honey instead of vinegar. We had a good morning in the studio. We got a lot of work done and then..."

When he didn't finish his sentence, Melissa peered at him. "Then what?"

Briggs made a funny face before he said, "I had a therapy appointment."

"You did?" That took her by surprise. He hadn't said anything about it earlier. "How did it go?"

"Pretty good, I think. He gave me some advice on what to do if my magic flares out of control again."

Melissa wanted to ask more but didn't. She'd never gone to therapy, but she imagined it would be intense. Especially for someone with Briggs's history. "That's great, Briggs." She lightened her tone and added, "I hope it works better than the potions."

He chuckled. "You and me both."

When they made it to town, Briggs parked in front of the new restaurant, the Elegant Cauldron, and then hurried over to open her door for her. "I hope you're hungry, because after the day I had, I'm starving."

"I could definitely eat," she said.

With his hand on the small of her back, he led her into the enchanted restaurant.

The door opened seemingly by itself the moment they stepped onto the short red carpet that was just outside the door. The entrance was dark, making Melissa hesitate, but when she got a whiff of the delicious scents inside, her mouth started to water and her feet began to move on their own.

As soon as she crossed the threshold, candles flickered to life and a woman dressed in a purple velvet dress and ornate lace-up, knee-high boots appeared before them.

"Mr. Williams," she said. "You're right on time. Your table is ready for you. Right this way."

Twinkle lights were strung along the walls and across the ceiling, giving the charming restaurant a beautiful glow. And when they got to their table, the chairs moved out all on their own. As Melissa was taking her seat, the chair scooted in to just the right distance for her to enjoy her meal.

"This is fun," she said, enjoying the special magical touches the witches had added to make dinner just a little bit more unique. "It's beautiful, too," she added as she took in the gorgeous tapestries on the walls that depicted various potions, herbs, and the ethereal witches who worked with them.

"Good evening," a waiter in a green crushed velvet suit said. "Can I bring you something to drink?"

Melissa frowned. "Do you have a wine menu?"

"Of course." He snapped his fingers, and suddenly a floating chalkboard appeared right next to their table with a list of wines by the glass and the bottle.

"Nice touch," Briggs said.

The waiter smiled. "Thanks. That was my idea."

"Can I have the Italian red?" Melissa asked.

"Absolutely. Do you want a bottle or a glass?"

"Bring the bottle," Briggs said.

"Good choice." The waiter didn't write it down or make a note of it anywhere. He just snapped his fingers again, and the wine list was replaced with the food menus. He rattled off a few specials and then said he'd be right back with their wine.

Once he was out of earshot, Melissa eyed her date. "Are you trying to get me drunk?"

"No," he said with a soft chuckle. "Not unless you want to."

"Tempting," she said. "But I do have to get up and leave early tomorrow."

"That's unfortunate. I already miss waking up and making you breakfast."

She winked at him. "I'm pretty sure you miss what happens *before* breakfast."

"That, too," he said, his eyes glinting with mischief.

The wine glasses and bottle appeared out of nowhere. They watched as the bottle rose in the air and poured wine into their glasses. Then Melissa's rose and hovered right over her plate. She took it, tasted the wine, and said, "It's delicious."

A mysterious voice sounded out of thin air. "Excellent. Enjoy."

Melissa smirked. "Is this just their way of keeping their staff costs down?"

"Maybe." Briggs glanced around, eyeing all the magic that was happening around them. "It is charming, though, right?"

"Very."

They spent the rest of the evening at the restaurant being delighted by the magical touches, but the real show was the food. Melissa had never had a more flavorful risotto. Briggs raved about his glazed duck. And then there was dessert. The key lime pie cheesecake was heaven. Pure heaven.

By the time they left, Melissa was starting to wonder if they'd charmed the food, too. Everything was so good, it must have been made with just a touch of magic.

"That was wonderful," Melissa said once they were back in the truck.

"And I didn't even get you drunk." He winked at her.

"Almost, but not quite," she said. "I can't believe we didn't finish the bottle."

"I didn't want you to accuse me of taking advantage of you," he said as he turned onto the highway that led out of town toward the mountains to the east.

"Is that right?" She peered out the windshield at the moonlit night. "Where are we headed now?"

"Just a nice little spot with a pretty view."

"Are you taking me to make-out point?" she asked.

"Would it be a problem if I did?"

"No." She leaned toward him, and this time it was Melissa who took his hand in hers. "I think I'd like a little alone time with you."

That sexy half smile was back, and Melissa felt a tingle of anticipation run up her spine, making her feel like she was seventeen again.

It wasn't long before he pulled off the highway and drove a couple miles back into the woods. When he finally stopped, they were overlooking a small lake that had the mountain behind it and the moon high overhead.

"Come on," he said as he climbed out of the cab of the truck.

"We're getting out?" she asked as he pulled her door open.

Once she was on her feet, he led her to the back of his truck and helped her climb in.

She laughed when she saw the two sleeping bags that had been zippered together. "You weren't kidding."

"Nope." He climbed up after her and then slipped his arms into her coat and pulled her to him. "I missed you, Melissa."

"I missed you, too," she breathed as his mouth brushed over her bare collarbone.

"Tell me I can have you, right here under the stars," he whispered.

Her body was lit with fire, and all she could do was nod.

An hour later, as they lay in the sleeping bags staring up

at the stars, Melissa said, "I wish we could live in this moment forever."

He trailed his fingers through her curls. "Me, too."

They stared up at the sky, both of them content just to be with each other. And when a shooting star appeared, Briggs just held her tighter and said, "It's always the small moments that stay with you."

Melissa wanted to laugh. "You call this a small moment?"

He glanced down at her and chuckled. "Okay, maybe a quiet moment."

"For now, anyway," she teased and then rose up to kiss him. They got lost in each other again, and by the time she told him it was time to go, the sun was just about to rise.

He sighed softly, kissed her one last time before they got dressed, and then took her home.

Briggs walked her to the door, and just before she went in, he said, "I think it's safe to say we're dating now."

"After one date?" she asked with a raised eyebrow.

"One *epic* date," he corrected. "I know you're supposed to be my fiancée, but I think maybe I'd like to be your boyfriend first."

"Boyfriend?" she asked with a grin.

"Yeah. Are you okay with that?"

Melissa stepped in, gave him a soft kiss on the lips, and said, "Yeah, I'm more than okay with that."

CHAPTER 18

Melissa practically floated into her house. Her date with Briggs had been nothing short of perfect. A good meal, great sex under the stars, and then they'd made their relationship official. She knew Briggs had baggage, but who didn't? And he was working on it. What more could she ask for?

If she had her way, she wouldn't be going out of town for the weekend. Unfortunately, that's when most of the vineyards she needed to visit were open, so she worked around their schedules. Traveling had never bothered her before. In fact, she quite liked it. Or at least she *had* liked it. In that moment, all Melissa wanted to do was change her clothes and then head right over to Briggs's place.

Instead, she hurried upstairs and jumped into the shower.

Once she was dressed and finished packing, Melissa headed back downstairs to grab a quick breakfast. But when she stepped into her kitchen, she froze. There were dishes everywhere, and flour was all over one of the counters.

She ground her teeth and scanned the mess. It looked as if Kassie had made—and burned—a batch of cookies. Plus, she'd cooked something in a frying pan that now had a crusty layer of black debris stuck to the bottom.

If there was one thing she couldn't stand in her house, it was a messy kitchen. Melissa had half a mind to barge into Kassie's room and demand she clean up her mess immediately, but she didn't have any faith that the younger woman even had the skills to clean anything.

With a scowl on her face, she put a kitchen apron on and got to work. By the time she wiped up the last of the flour that covered her counter, she had worked up a slight sweat and was more than ready to evict her house guest.

"Oh my gosh!" Kassie said as she appeared in the kitchen, wearing the shortest sleep shorts and a tiny formfitting camisole. "You didn't need to clean this up. I was going to do it this morning."

"Too late now," Melissa snapped. "I couldn't just leave it like that, much less find even an inch of counter space to prepare my breakfast."

Kassie winced. "I'm sorry. I honestly didn't think you'd be back until later."

Melissa turned around to stare at the woman. "Listen, Kassie." She blew out a breath. "Just clean up as you go in the kitchen, okay? I can't stand to even have dishes just sitting in the sink."

"Right. Sorry." She walked over to the counter and

pulled out a plastic container. "I made these for you… as a thank you."

"What?" Melissa asked as she stared at the plastic bowl.

"They're peanut butter cookies. I thought you could take them for the road. But if you don't like peanut butter then—"

"No, I do," Melissa said, feeling a little bit like a jerk. "Thank you. That was very kind."

"It was nothing. Baking helps me relax. So does the wine I had last night, which is why I didn't get the kitchen cleaned. I am sorry." Kassie chewed on her bottom lip and then started to retreat back down the hall.

"Kassie!" Melissa called.

"Yeah?" She turned back, meeting Melissa's gaze.

"I'm sorry I snapped at you. Mornings aren't always my best time of day."

"Don't worry about it. I am a messy cook. Have a good trip." She offered a tentative smile and then disappeared into the guest room.

Feeling like a heel, Melissa tucked the cookies into her bag, grabbed a bagel and a to-go cup of coffee, and then headed out. She only prayed that her house was still livable when she returned.

BRIGGS WOKE from a nap on his couch to a loud knock on his door. He rubbed the sleep out of his eyes and smiled to himself, hoping it was a surprise visit from his gorgeous girlfriend.

"Briggs!" an all-too-familiar voice called through the door. "Are you in there? Your truck is here. Open up."

He groaned. Kassie Kinny was at his door. How did she even get there? Did she find a way to rent another car? Get a ride from someone? He wiped the sleep from his eyes and rolled off the couch.

"Kassie, what are you doing here?" he asked when he opened his front door.

"Hi." She wore a shy smile as her cheeks flushed pink. "Sorry to just show up without calling. I just… needed to talk to you."

He swallowed a sigh, noted a blue bike that was leaning against his porch railing, and opened the door wider to let her in. "Do you need something to drink? It's a pretty long ride from Melissa's house."

"Yes, please." She followed him into his kitchen and sat on one of the barstools as she waited for her water.

"Are you hungry? There's fruit in the basket."

"No thanks," she said. "Water's fine."

Briggs handed her the glass and then just stood there in his kitchen watching her. It was the weekend, and while they usually didn't keep normal business hours for recording, Austin had told them to take both days off and they'd start fresh on Monday. Briggs had been looking forward to a break from her. To reset and put her out of his mind for a few days.

But here she was, sitting in his kitchen, taking up space he'd wanted to reclaim as his own.

She sipped the water and stared past him out his back window.

"I don't mean to be rude," Briggs said, "but what brings you all the way over here, Kassie?"

She put the glass down. "I came to apologize."

He raised both eyebrows, shocked. Had he ever heard her say she was sorry? As far as he could recall, those words had only ever been muttered when she was being sarcastic or passive aggressive. "You are? For what exactly, barging into my life? Posting lies about me and King? Being a general pain in the ass?"

She winced. "All of the above, I guess." She finally met his gaze. "I know I shouldn't have just assumed you'd let me stay here. The truth is that I'm dead broke."

"Yeah, you said that." He crossed his arms over his chest and waited for her to continue.

"It's my mom. She got behind on rent and is in debt to some pretty bad people. I ended up helping her out, and now I'm struggling to stay afloat. The tour money wasn't as good as I thought it was going to be. The expenses… Well, I wasn't as careful as I should have been, and now I'm in a bind."

"Did you come here to ask me for money?" he asked, narrowing his eyes at her. Was that the reason she was telling him all of this?

"Money?" she parroted, looking surprised and a little hurt. "Gods, no. I'm not that crass."

He wasn't so sure about that, but he was relieved he wasn't going to have to shut her down.

"I'm just explaining why I barged my way into your life. I told myself that you wouldn't mind if I stayed with you. We spent so much time together while we worked on the last album, and you were so easygoing I guess I thought we'd just go back to that. Then when I found out about Melissa, I was jealous and panicked because I didn't know what I was going to do."

"Okay," he said, not sure what else to say.

"I just wanted to tell you that I appreciate your help. And Melissa's, too. I like her. She's good for you."

"She is," he agreed.

"I've just been worried about paying bills. And now my mom is calling all the time, asking for more, and I just need this album to work." She fingered the hem of her sparkly T-shirt. "I suppose I just wanted to make sure we can put all of that behind us and knock this record out."

"Sure, I can do that," Briggs said, hoping that she was being sincere. He wasn't one for holding onto petty grievances. He was never going to be besties with Kassie Kinny, but he could be civil. Maybe even friendly if she returned to acting like the woman he'd known back in LA. He just didn't care for the fame-hungry version of her.

"Good." She let out a sigh of relief. After a beat, she asked, "How do you think the album is going?"

"Pretty good," he said honestly. "That song with King is a banger. I'll be shocked if it doesn't get massive airplay."

"What about the rest?" She stared at him intently as if she really cared what he thought.

So far, he'd kept most of his opinions to himself. He hadn't wanted to engage with Kassie any more than he had to. But since she seemed sincere, he said, "I prefer the songs that are packed with soul-baring honesty."

She looked a little pale but nodded. "I'm guessing your favorite is 'Stripped.'"

"Yes." He nodded. "It gets right to the heart of how vulnerable one has to be to bare their soul to another person. And how painful that can be if one is rejected. The song is haunting and beautiful. And raw. It's the kind of song that wins awards."

"It's the hardest one for me to sing," she said, her eyes glinting with unshed tears.

"That's how you know it's honest," he said softly.

"I suppose." She closed her eyes for a moment, appearing to collect herself. "But I can't have an entire album of songs like that. I'd have to be committed by the time I was done."

"Of course not, but you can still be honest and raw in the most upbeat pop songs. That's what makes them interesting."

"I suppose." She pursed her lips and then pulled her phone out of her back pocket. "Will you listen to something for me?"

"Of course." He sat down next to her and waited.

Kassie scrolled through her phone until she found the right voice note. The snippet she played was a rough cut of just her voice and a piano. It was an up-tempo number, and the lyrics were about flying. Only she didn't mean on a plane. The song was about emotional highs and lows and how she lived to fly, even if she had to lie to herself to do it.

"What do you think?" she asked.

Briggs's brain had immediately snapped into production mode. He stood. "Come on. Let's get to the studio. I have a few ideas."

"But Austin said to take the weekend to regroup," she said, looking both hopeful and a little apprehensive.

"This is regrouping. Let's go." He grabbed his keys and strode out the door. On his way, he grabbed the bike and threw it in the back of his truck. "When we're done, I'll drop you off back at Melissa's."

Kassie's grin lit up her entire face as she climbed into his truck. Then she said, "This is what I envisioned when I decided to come to Keating Hollow to record my album."

He glanced at her as he started the truck. "Collaborating?"

She nodded. "You always did get me and my song writing."

He let out a humorless snort. "You should have just said that in the beginning. We could have avoided a lot of this drama."

"Even after all those texts I sent while I was on the road?" she asked.

He had to admit that he was surprised she acknowledged that faux pas. Chuckling, he said, "Maybe not. But let's just put that behind us and make the best record we can, okay?"

"Okay." She held out her fist to him. Briggs laughed as he touched his fist to hers just like he would with King.

And for just a moment, he decided that maybe they could find a way back to being friends.

CHAPTER 19

"What do you think?" Briggs asked King. They were sitting in the studio, listening to a playback of Kassie's new song, "Flying High." On the way to the studio, Briggs had called Austin to get permission to try some new things. He'd known his boss would be cool about it, so he wasn't surprised when Austin had told him to go for it. And then when King had called while Kassie was in the middle of working out a lyric, Briggs had asked him to come give his input.

The three of them had been in the studio for hours and had just finished the song.

King turned to Briggs. "It's brilliant. That riff you put in just before the bridge is effing incredible. I'm jealous it's not on my album."

"It's soooo good," Kassie said from the booth. "I love it!"

Briggs felt a deep sense of accomplishment. His job was

sound mixing, and while he'd certainly helped King work out arrangements with his songs occasionally, he'd never really taken on the role of producer before. But after years of working in the studio with Austin and King, he'd been bound to pick up some skills, right? "It was a true collaboration," he said.

"I agree, but you're the one who did most of the musical arrangements. I just helped smooth out the lyrics," King said. "The magic is in the production and the passion that Kassie brings to it."

"Thanks for that," Kassie said softly.

Briggs knew there was still tension between the two of them, but as always, when everything was clicking in the studio, all the BS just seemed to fade into the background. There was nothing more healing than when two artists were able to come together to make something special.

"And thanks for coming in today," Kassie told King. "You helped make a good sound great."

"You're just lucky Sadie was working today, otherwise, I'd have blown you both off," King said.

Kassie walked out of the booth and stood right next to King as she looked down at him. "Can I ask you something?"

"That depends on the question," he said warily.

Kassie rolled her eyes. "Come on, I'm not going to ask to move in or anything."

Briggs chuckled softly and was relieved that they were in a place where they could joke about such things.

"Okay, out with it," King said.

"Why does Sadie still work at the brewery? You two have

a hit record. Surely she's making enough so that she can just focus on music," Kassie mused.

"She gets asked that a lot," King said. "Sadie continues working there because she likes it, and the Townsends are like family to her. They're flexible and let her have time off whenever she needs it. Plus, it takes the pressure off *having* to make a living with music."

"It must be nice to have a place that feels like family to fall back on," Kassie said wistfully.

Briggs thought about what she'd said earlier, about how she was struggling even though, by most standards, she'd had a successful first album. It just reinforced the fact that making money in music was a tough road to go down. King had certainly had his share of ups and downs over the years, too.

King just nodded and then stood. "I better get going. Congrats, Kassie. The song is fire."

Kassie wrapped her arms around him in an impromptu hug.

King stiffened, giving Briggs a deer-in-the-headlights look. When she didn't let go, he tentatively returned the hug and then stepped back awkwardly. "Okay, well… time to go. Briggs, I'll call you later."

Briggs nodded at him as he stifled a chuckle. Then he looked at Kassie. "Want to get something to eat?"

"Sure." She beamed at him and then chattered happily about the song all the way to the Cozy Cave.

"I'm buying," Kassie said as they looked over their menus.

"That's not necessary," Briggs said. "I invited you."

"No, no. With everything you did today, it's only right that I treat."

"Forget it," he insisted. "I've been where you are. I'll pay. You can treat me when you finally get your number one hit or something."

She gave him a grateful smile and nodded. "Okay. You're on."

They talked music the entire meal, and when they walked out of the restaurant, both of them were relaxed and happy.

"I can ride to Melissa's from here," Kassie said when they got to his truck.

"It's no big deal to just drop you off," he said, already climbing into the cab. "Besides, it's dark and pretty cold out. Just get in."

She didn't argue.

When they got to Melissa's house, Briggs stared up at her bedroom window, wishing she was there. He'd missed her today. Even though he'd enjoyed his time in the studio, he still wished he could end the day wrapped in her arms. The memory of her cuddled up next to him in his sleeping bag the night before brought a smile to his face.

"Thank you for such a great day, Briggs," Kassie said, placing her hand on his thigh.

He stared at her hand and frowned. "Sure, Kas. I enjoyed it, too." Then he quickly jumped out of the cab and retrieved the bike from the back. "Where does Melissa keep this?"

"In the garage. This way." She led him to the side door, opened it for him, and flicked on the light.

The garage was tidy, with plastic bins stacked on a rack on one side and a toolbox on the other. It didn't surprise him. Melissa was the orderly type. He rolled the bike over to where a helmet was hanging on the wall and then turned to Kassie. "I'll see you Monday."

"You don't have to go," she said as she stepped in front of him, blocking him from leaving. "I can make hot cocoa and we can talk more music by the fireplace."

"That's not—"

"Come on, Briggs." She stared up at him with her big eyes and pouty lips. "We had such a good day. You don't want that to end do you?" She reached up to brush a lock of hair out of his eyes. "Our chemistry—"

Briggs grabbed her hand, stopping her. "There's no chemistry," he insisted. "We had a good day in the studio. Let's just leave it at that."

Undeterred, Kassie placed her other hand on his pec and lightly trailed her fingers over his well-defined muscle. "We both know how good we are together. Let's not deny ourselves this night, Briggs. I've missed you."

He stepped back, feeling that tingle of magic spark at his spine. He pictured Melissa's smiling face and forced out, "I said no."

"Oh, come on," Kassie said with a sigh. "What's wrong with having a little fun? You're not married... yet. And the little woman isn't even here. Don't tell me you're not attracted to me. You weren't faking it back in LA."

Briggs wondered what Melissa would say if she heard Kassie throwing herself at him. He imagined his girlfriend throwing her out of the house and telling her not to let the door hit her on the ass on the way out. He chuckled softly, shook his head, and then moved for the door. When she darted in front of him again, he grabbed her by her arms, picked her up, and physically moved her.

Once he was outside, he peered back in and said, "Don't ever do that again. Understand?"

"A girl has to take her shot," Kassie said flippantly and then hurried into the house.

Briggs couldn't believe that they'd had an entire day of normalcy, and he'd actually thought that they were moving past the issues Kassie had brought with her to Keating Hollow. Then she'd had to go and ruin it right at the end.

Did she have no decency? Melissa was letting her stay at her house, and Kassie couldn't refrain from hitting on Melissa's fiancé. Well, fake fiancé, but Kassie didn't know that. It appeared that leopards really didn't ever change their spots.

Briggs would do well to remember that.

Feeling frustrated with how the day ended, Briggs climbed back into his truck and headed home. He took a long hot shower, climbed into bed, and then called Melissa. "Hey, gorgeous."

"Hey yourself," she said, and he could hear the smile in her voice. "How was your day?"

"Pretty great, actually. Or it was right up until about an hour ago," he said.

"What happened?"

He explained that Kassie had come over to apologize

and how that led to working in the studio and going to dinner afterward.

"That sounds pretty amazing so far," Melissa said, seeming perfectly fine with him spending the day with his ex-situationship. "What ruined it?"

"Kassie," he said bluntly. "I took her back to your place, and she hit on me pretty hard."

There was silence on the other end.

"Melissa?"

"I'm here," she said, her tone flat. "That woman is—"

"A snake?" he offered.

She chuckled. "Yes. Just when you think she might be sincere, she turns around and does something that vile. It's pretty pathetic, but then so is texting someone eight thousand messages when they never text you back."

"True," he agreed.

"How did you handle it? Did sparks fly? The kind that burns things down, I mean. Not the passionate kind."

He laughed. "Almost, but I told you my therapist gave me some tools to use, and I was able to get myself out of there before we had to rebuild your garage."

"That's good," she said, sounding relieved. "I'm really happy your therapist was able to help."

"Same. Now tell me about your day. Are all the wine clients happy?"

"Most of them." Melissa spent the next ten minutes telling him all about her favorite winery and how she wanted to take him down the coast once the weather warmed up.

Briggs happily listened, imagining spending a nice warm day with her, touring her favorite wineries and listening to her talk about distribution and wine pairings and all the boring things she loved about her job.

It just seemed so normal. And that sounded just about perfect to him.

CHAPTER 20

Melissa loaded the back of her Audi with a couple of cases of her favorite wine and then climbed into her vehicle to make the trip back to Keating Hollow. It was Sunday afternoon, and she'd managed to see all her clients ahead of schedule. She was hoping to get back into town before dinner so that she could spend the evening with Briggs.

In fact, she planned to go straight to his house, because if she had to deal with Kassie, she wasn't sure she could keep her cool. The audacity of that woman to hit on Briggs while staying at Melissa's house—for free no less—was mind-boggling.

Who did that?

Entitled trash. That's who.

She knew that the other woman had some life issues, but that didn't excuse her behavior, and Melissa wasn't inclined to give her any sort of pass.

The afternoon sun was glinting off the Pacific Ocean when a call rang through the Bluetooth on her vehicle's dash. Sadie's name flashed across the screen, making Melissa smile. She hadn't talked to her friend since she and Briggs had made things official, and she couldn't wait to share the news.

Melissa hit Accept and said, "Hey, bestie. How's your Sunday?"

"Where are you?" Sadie asked, sounding stressed.

"On 101, headed home. Why? Where are you?"

"At the sheriff's station." Sadie's voice caught when she said, "Briggs has been arrested."

Melissa was so distracted she almost ran right off the road. She quickly corrected her steering and then pulled off to the side of the road and slammed the car into Park. "What do you mean he's been arrested? Why? What did he do?"

"They think he abducted Kassie."

Ringing sounded in Melissa's ears, and she was certain that she hadn't heard her friend right. "Say that again?"

"Kassie is missing, and they think that Briggs did it. Melissa, you have to get back here. King and I are very worried. It doesn't look good."

"Tell me everything," Melissa demanded as she pulled back onto the highway and laid into the gas pedal.

"Well, so far all we know is that there was a small explosion at the studio earlier this morning. There's a partial video of Kassie being hauled off by someone taller than her. They found your bike and a credit card with Briggs's name on it at the scene."

Melissa's heart got caught in her throat. "That's..."

"Not good," Sadie finished for her.

"What does Briggs say?" There had to be a reasonable explanation. There just had to be. Kassie could have taken Briggs's credit card. She was struggling, after all.

"We don't know. King hasn't been able to talk to him. He's working on getting him a lawyer, but with it being Sunday, he's having a hard time finding someone." Sadie sniffed. "King is taking this really hard."

"I can imagine." Tears stung Melissa's eyes, but she did her best to swallow her emotions. This was no time to panic. Until she knew more, she was going to assume that the law had the wrong guy. "What about Kassie? Do we know anything? Why she was at the studio, who she was with, when she went missing?"

"No. I went to your house. All her stuff is still there. And I found a full cup of tea that still had the tea bag in it with the honey pot sitting next to it. Plus there is toast sitting in the toaster. If I had to guess, I'd say she took off in a hurry."

That likely meant she went to town to meet someone she knew at the studio. Where she'd been the previous day with Briggs and King. But Briggs had been upset with her the night before, and his solution to dealing with her was to ignore her or stay away from her.

A voice in Melissa's head chimed in with, *What if she convinced him to work on another song and he lost control?*

Unfortunately, that was a very real possibility.

"Just hang tight. I'm on my way," Melissa said. "And Sadie?"

"Yes?"

"Call me if you learn anything new. Anything at all."

"I will," Sadie promised.

Melissa ended the call and sped up, praying that she wouldn't run into any highway patrol on the way.

THE DRIVE back to Keating Hollow had been excruciating. Thankfully, Melissa had managed to avoid being pulled over, but it had been a close call a couple of times. As soon as she got back into town, she headed straight for the sheriff's office.

"Can I help you?" a pretty redhead named Clarissa asked from behind the receptionist's desk.

Melissa knew who the clerk was just because she'd grown up in Keating Hollow, but the two weren't close. "Yes, Clarissa, I'm here to see Briggs Williams."

Clarissa frowned as she tapped on her computer keys. "Your name is Melissa, right?"

"Yes. Melissa Bensen."

The receptionist nodded. "I thought so. I'm sorry, Melissa, but Briggs isn't allowed visitors yet. I can put your name on the list and let you know when you're approved."

"When will that be?" Melissa asked, feeling as if she were going to come right out of her skin.

"Honestly, likely not until tomorrow. Nothing really happens around here on Sundays. I'm only working because of all the commotion. They needed someone to man the desk. I tell ya, I was not ready to come back to work. I had plans to—"

Impatient, Melissa cut her off. "I'm sorry your Sunday was ruined. Can I talk to the sheriff?"

"Sheriff Baker is busy right now, but I can let him know you're waiting," she said.

"Please. It's important," Melissa said and then went to sit in one of the uncomfortable plastic chairs. While she was waiting, she texted Sadie. *Where are you?*

No reply.

Melissa rose from the chair and dialed Sadie's number.

It went straight to voice mail.

She wanted to scream in frustration, but she kept her cool and tapped out another message to her friend. *I'm at the sheriff's station. Call me as soon as you get this.*

"Ms. Benson?" a male voice asked from behind her.

Melissa spun around to find Sheriff Baker standing there in plain clothes. "Sheriff," she said. "I need to talk to Briggs Williams."

"Visiting hours are over," he said matter-of-factly. "But even if they weren't, he's still being processed. After his arraignment tomorrow, if he doesn't make bail, you can set up a time to see him them."

"If he doesn't make bail?" she parroted. "*If?*"

"He's been arrested for a serious crime, Ms. Benson. I can't predict what the judge will decide."

"What evidence do you have that Briggs abducted Kassie?" she demanded. "I know him. He'd never do anything like that. I'm telling you there's been a mistake."

He gave her a look of pity. One that said he'd heard it all before.

Melissa was so frustrated that her eyes began to burn

with tears again. "You have to tell me something. Anything to help me understand."

"Why don't we go talk in my office," he said as he placed his hand on her elbow and started to guide her through the station.

The unease in her gut only intensified as they made their way down the hall.

When they got to a small windowless office that was as sterile and generic as she could imagine, he gestured for her to enter before him. He followed and shut the door, leaving them in the small room with florescent lighting glaring in her eyes.

"This isn't *your* office, is it?" she asked.

"No, but it affords us some privacy." He opened a drawer and took out a yellow legal pad and a pen. "Before we get started, can you tell me what your relationship to Briggs Williams is?"

"I'm his girlfriend," she said.

He wrote that down and asked, "How long have you been dating?"

Melissa frowned. "I'm not sure why that matters."

"I'm just trying to get a clear picture of who Briggs Williams is and who he spends time with. That's all."

"I thought you were going to give me some insight on what's going on with Briggs, not interrogate me," Melissa said, ready to get up and leave.

"I promise you, this isn't an interrogation," he said, not unkindly. "I really do want to make sure we have the right person in custody. And if it turns out we don't, I'd like to get him released as soon as possible."

When he put it that way, Melissa supposed she could cooperate a little. "We've only been dating for about a week, but I've known him for much longer. Briggs is King McGrath's best friend. King dates my best friend, Sadie Lewis, so I've spent a lot of time with all of them over the past few months."

It felt weird to say that she'd only been with Briggs for a week. In her heart, it felt like much longer. That was probably because she'd been crushing on him for ages. She just hadn't let herself act on it because she didn't want to get hurt if he wasn't willing to commit.

"Were you aware of any hard feelings or conflict between Mr. Williams and Ms. Kinny?"

Melissa stared at him for a long moment. "I think we're done here."

He raised his eyebrows curiously. "Is that a yes?"

"It's a no comment. And I really don't appreciate you pretending like you're going to answer some of my questions and then treating me like I'm a suspect or witness to something. I've been out of town the last two days. I don't know anything." Melissa got up and swept out of the room with her chest aching and a sob caught in her throat.

She hurried past Clarissa and ran outside, gasping for breath.

"Melissa!" Sadie called as she ran forward and wrapped her arms around her. "Are you okay? What happened?"

"The sheriff. Questions. I can't—"

"It's okay," Sadie soothed. "Come on. Let's get you out of here."

"But Briggs…"

"King found a lawyer. Lorna White is already working on the fastest way to get him out of here. Apparently she has a judge friend who can expedite the arraignment. Come on. King will keep us updated. Let's go."

Melissa let herself be led away by her friend, but with each step away from the sheriff's department, she felt like she was leaving a piece of herself behind.

CHAPTER 21

"Mr. Williams," Deputy Sheriff Hunt said as he opened the jail cell. "Come with me."

Briggs rose from the hard bench without a word and followed the man past the four other cells that were empty. Apparently, Keating Hollow wasn't a hotbed of crime. Or at least it wasn't until Kassie had gone missing that morning.

Bile rose up in the back of his throat. It wasn't so much that he was worried for himself, though he had to admit that being arrested hadn't been on his bingo card. It was that Kassie appeared to have been abducted, and since everyone thought that Briggs had done it, no one was looking for the real perpetrator. The thought made him sick to his stomach. No matter how much Kassie got under his skin at times, he definitely didn't want to see anything bad happen to her. And if she was being held against her will… He ground his teeth together so hard that his jaw ached.

"Your lawyer is waiting for you in here," Hunt said, opening a door and waving him inside.

"What lawyer?" Briggs asked. It was the first time he'd spoken to anyone since they'd arrested him that morning.

The deputy sheriff didn't respond. He just waited for Briggs to enter and then closed the door, leaving Briggs alone with the woman who already occupied the room.

"Mr. Williams, I'm Lorna White." The woman with long gray hair and serious blue eyes stood and held out her hand. "Your friend King McGrath hired me on your behalf. I'm here to help if that's acceptable to you."

Briggs said a silent thank you to King and shook the woman's hand. "It is. If King hired you, then I'm good with that."

"Excellent." She took her seat and opened a folder. "Let's get down to it, shall we?"

Briggs nodded and sat down across from her.

"First of all, do you know why you're here?" she asked.

"They said I was under arrest for the assault and abduction of Kassie Kinny," he recited in a flat tone.

"Yes, that's on the arrest warrant," she confirmed. "They have video of her being attacked outside the recording studio where you work early this morning." She checked the paperwork. "Says here the time stamp is 7:39 a.m. I haven't seen it yet, but the notes indicate that while Ms. Kinny is in full view, the video only portrays a partial back view of the attacker." She looked up from her notes. "Can you tell me where you were at 7:39 a.m. this morning?"

"At home in bed," he said.

"Was anyone there with you?"

RISE OF THE WITCH

"In my bed?" he asked but then quickly shook his head. "No. I was home alone. No one else was there."

"Okay, reasonable for a Sunday morning." She tapped her fingers on the table. "The arrest report indicates they found your credit card at the scene, and it appears the attacker was wearing a flannel shirt that matches one you've worn before."

Briggs frowned. "My credit card was there?"

"Yes. Your legal name is Brandon Williams, correct?"

He nodded. Briggs had changed his name once he'd gone to foster care. He didn't want to be reminded of the kid who'd spent his childhood getting his ass kicked by his father.

"There's a picture of it here." She turned the file around so he could see his credit card, the one he'd used just the night before at dinner, lying on the ground.

"I have zero idea how it got there. Honestly. I used it at dinner at the Cozy Cave last night and haven't touched it since," Briggs explained.

"Is it possible you forgot to grab it and left it at the restaurant?" Lorna asked.

"Maybe?" He frowned. "I don't know."

"I'll mark that as a yes. There are witnesses who say you were with Ms. Kinny on Saturday night. Is that true?"

"Yes." Briggs went on to explain that they'd spent the day in the studio and then went to get dinner before he dropped her off at Melissa's house that night. "I haven't seen or heard from her since."

"And there's no one who can verify that you were at home?"

He shook his head.

"Do you have security cameras that maybe recorded you coming and going?" she asked hopefully.

"I have cameras on my front and back doors," he said. "I can send you the clips if I ever get out of here."

"Okay, that's good," she said with a nod. "It won't stop speculation that you could have used a window, but it helps."

Briggs groaned.

"Don't get discouraged," she warned. "We're just getting started."

That was exactly what he was afraid of.

After she asked a bunch of questions about his relationship with Kassie, and then about his relationship with King and their shared history, she closed the file and leaned forward. "Here's the deal. As of now, they don't have anything but circumstantial evidence."

"They have my credit card at the scene," he said, feeling pretty defeated.

"That can be explained away," she said with a wave of her hand. "Maybe Kassie took it. You said she was having money issues. Desperate people do desperate things. The point is, there is no smoking gun, and no judge is going to keep you behind bars with only circumstantial evidence. Bail will likely be set low since you don't have any priors."

"Okay. When can I get out of here? Tonight?"

She shook her head. "Likely tomorrow morning. Right now, Sheriff Baker wants an interview with you since you refused to answer any questions without a lawyer present when they arrested you. Are you ready for that?"

He wasn't, but it wasn't like they were just going to escort him back to his cell. "Yeah, but I'm warning you now; I don't trust law enforcement, so I'm not likely to answer any questions at all."

"That's your right. And in this case, I think it's best." She stood. "I'll let the sheriff know we're ready."

A few minutes later, Sheriff Baker entered the tiny room along with Lorna. Briggs's lawyer sat next to him, and the sheriff took the seat across from them.

"Good evening, Mr. Williams," the sheriff said. "I'm hoping we can have a conversation to clear a few things up."

Briggs didn't respond.

Lorna cleared her throat. "My client has informed me that he'd like to exercise his First Amendment rights, Sheriff."

Drew Baker let out a tired sigh. "That is, of course, your right, Mr. Williams. But I want to assure you that I really am here to figure out what happened to Ms. Kinny."

"If that were true, you'd be out looking for whoever abducted her," Briggs said. "Not wasting your time with me."

"So you're saying that you did not meet up with Ms. Kinny this morning?" Drew asked.

"That's what I'm saying," Briggs said. He wasn't going to answer any questions about his relationship with Kassie or their past interaction, but he would make it clear they were making a mistake. "The longer you try to pin this on me, the longer Kassie remains in danger."

"Can you tell me how you know Ms. Kinny?" Baker asked.

Briggs paused and looked at Lorna. When she nodded, he said, "She's a singer. I work for the studio where she's recording."

"Okay. And is it fair to say that you were in a relationship with her at one time?"

"I have no comment on that," Briggs said.

"All right. Can you tell me about this TikTok video that was put out by Ms. Kinny? It heavily implies that you are involved in a relationship with King McGrath. Did you know about this?"

Briggs gave the sheriff a flat stare.

"No comment," Lorna answered for him.

Sheriff Baker went on to ask a number of questions about his involvement with Kassie, how long he'd known her, if he knew of anyone who might be a person of interest, as well as his whereabouts for the last forty-eight hours. He didn't answer any of them. Instead, he just said, "You've got the wrong man, Sheriff. If you're really worried about Kassie, you need to look elsewhere."

"That's what I'm trying to do, Mr. Williams," Baker said, sounding impatient now. "Your insistence on not speaking isn't going to help us find her."

"Perhaps I'd be more talkative if I hadn't been arrested," he said and then stood. "Can I go back to my cell now?"

The sheriff leaned back in his chair and nodded. "If you think of anything you think we should know, please don't hesitate to tell one of the deputies. I'll be here."

Briggs stood in the hallway with his lawyer and one of the deputies.

"I'll see you first thing in the morning," Lorna said. "King

McGrath has already said he'd cover any bail. With any luck, you'll be home tomorrow by lunchtime."

"Thank you," he said and then followed the deputy back to his cell.

After he heard the clanging of metal on metal, he sat on the bench and leaned against the cold cement wall. It was going to be one long night.

CHAPTER 22

Melissa clutched Sadie's hand as they walked into the courthouse in Eureka. King was just ahead of them, talking to Lorna White. The lawyer seemed to think that Briggs would be released shortly after the hearing, but Melissa was too nervous to get her hopes up.

She hadn't slept a wink the night before. All she could think about was Briggs sitting in a jail cell by himself with the worst-case scenarios running through his mind.

"It's going to be okay," Sadie said.

"You don't know that," Melissa whispered back. "What if the judge is a major jackass and sets a bail that King can't cover?" Goddess knew that Melissa didn't have a pile of money just sitting around. She had her house, but that was it.

"Look." Sadie pointed to a small group of people who

were standing off to the side. "Isn't that Yvette Townsend-Burton?"

"And that's Bronwyn from Mystyk Pizza," Melissa added. "Why are they here?" Her pulse kicked up a notch as her heart started to flutter with nerves. "You don't think they're here to testify against Briggs, do you?"

"Testify about what? That he helped Bronwyn put her restaurant back together and that he immediately called Yvette when the window was broken at her store?" Sadie asked, looking annoyed. "If they do that, then—"

"That's not why they're here," Lorna White said.

"King, good, you're already here," a man said from behind them.

Melissa spun and spotted Austin Steele, Briggs's boss.

King shook the man's hand and asked, "Do you have your statement?"

"What statement?" Melissa asked. "What's going on?" She hated feeling like she was in the dark.

"Lorna asked if there were any people in town who would write character statements for Briggs," King said. "I thought they'd just send the letters, but it looks like they cared enough to show up in person."

The judge entered the courtroom, and everyone scrambled to take their seats.

Melissa wanted to personally thank Austin, Yvette, and Bronwyn, but court was starting and all she could do was wait to see what happened next.

The judge called everyone to order and then listened to the charges against Briggs. Aggravated assault and false imprisonment. The evidence was presented, and then it was time for Briggs's lawyer to talk.

"Your Honor," Lorna White said. "The state has taken quite a bit of liberty with the letter of the law. There is zero evidence that my client has attacked or imprisoned Ms. Kinny. In fact, no one even knows where she is. It is possible that she just left town, even though that is unlikely. And the video proof they have of her attack shows only the back of someone's shoulder. There are no identifying marks that point to my client. Everything you've heard today is completely circumstantial. I dare say that if this case goes to trial, there is a strong chance it will be thrown out altogether."

"What about the motive, Ms. White?" the judge asked.

"So far, we've only heard that Ms. Kinny and Mr. Williams had some disagreements that resulted in magical flares from Mr. Williams. By all accounts, Mr. Williams has done everything in his power to rectify those actions, including seeking therapy. The business owners of Keating Hollow and Mr. Williams's employer are here to share that they have no ill will toward him. In fact, they strongly believe that he is an asset to their community."

The judge looked over at Austin, Yvette, and Bronwyn. "I have the letters from the business owners. Do they have more to add, or will I just get more of the same?"

"I can't speak for them," Lorna said. "But they took it upon themselves to show up here today to support him."

"I see. Okay, I've heard enough," the judge said.

"Wait!" Yvette called as Bronwyn stood. Chatter broke out around the courtroom until the judge banged her gavel.

"Quiet down now. I've already made my decision." She turned to the state's representative. "Mr. Vickers, it is my opinion that your evidence is flimsy at best. As Ms. White pointed out, everything you've presented is circumstantial. Mr. Williams cannot be identified as the attacker on the video, and there is zero proof of false imprisonment. I suggest you rethink these charges. In light of this, I'm releasing Mr. Williams with no bond. He'll be required to return to court *if* his case even makes it back onto the docket. You are dismissed."

Briggs stood and stared at his lawyer for a long moment. Then after a few words from her, he smiled.

Melissa darted out of her seat and ran over to him, flinging herself into his arms. "Oh my gods, Briggs. I was so worried about you."

His arms came around her as he buried his face into her shoulder. "You came."

"Of course I did," she said as she pulled back to look him in the eye. "Did you really think I wouldn't?"

"I don't know," he said with a tired laugh. "You could have thought I was guilty."

She scoffed. "I have faith in you even if you don't have any in me."

He gave her a horrified look. "That's not what I meant. I just—"

"Forget it," she said and hugged him again.

King and Sadie were there, both of them clapping him on the back in support.

Briggs hugged King, and with his voice thick with emotion, he said, "Thanks, man."

"No need to thank me," King said. "Let's just get out of here so you can get home and shower. I know it's only been about twenty-four hours, but you look like you slept in the gutter."

He didn't look *that* bad, Melissa mused, but he did look tired.

"Give me just a minute," he said and then went over to talk to Yvette and Bronwyn.

Melissa slumped against Sadie. "That went about as well as we could have expected, right?"

Lorna White cleared her throat and answered before Sadie could say anything. "It did. The only thing better would be if the charges were dismissed altogether. But the case is so new that I'm not surprised the judge let them stand. They'll need a hell of a lot better evidence to get much further though. The best thing to do now is pray that Kassie is found… safe." She nodded at King. "Tell Briggs I'll be in touch."

Once Briggs was finished talking to the business owners from Keating Hollow, he returned to Melissa's side and said, "Take me home."

MELISSA PLACED four bowls on Briggs's dining room table and called, "Lunch is ready." While Briggs had been in the shower, she'd searched his kitchen for something she could make them all to eat. She'd finally settled on macaroni and cheese. As far as she was concerned, they could all use a little comfort food.

"I'll get the drinks," Sadie said.

Melissa stared at the table and then blinked. Her mind had been elsewhere, and she'd completely forgotten about that. She smiled at her friend. "Thanks."

King walked in and took a seat. A few seconds later, Briggs appeared. His hair was still wet from his shower, but he looked a thousand times better than he had at the courthouse. As he walked past Melissa, he gave her a kiss on the cheek.

"Sit down and eat," Sadie ordered as she placed sodas on the table. "All of you must be starving."

To be honest, Melissa wasn't all that hungry. She'd been so upset about Briggs being arrested, she hadn't had an appetite. And so far, it hadn't returned.

She was thrilled that Briggs was back home, but she couldn't stop thinking about Kassie. "What do you think happened yesterday morning?" she asked. "With Kassie, I mean."

The other three looked up from their bowls and stared at her. No one had an answer.

"Do you think it was some random stranger or someone she knew?" Melissa pressed.

"I'd guess someone she knew," King offered. "She rode your bike to the studio at like seven in the morning while leaving her breakfast untouched in your kitchen. Seems she got called away, right?"

"It definitely looked like that," Sadie confirmed. "Her tea was still steeping, and there was toast in the toaster."

"Who would want to meet her at the studio?" Briggs

asked. "If it wasn't me or King, the only other person it could be is Austin."

"Austin wouldn't call her in on a Sunday, would he?" Melissa asked. "Isn't he pretty strict about spending the weekends with his wife, Brinn?" That was what Briggs had told her when she asked if he ever had to work on Saturdays or Sundays.

"No," Briggs said. "He never comes in unless it's on the schedule. He told me once that part of the reason he moved to Keating Hollow was so that he didn't feel pressured to work all the time. The only reason I can see him going in was if he really wanted to listen to the song we recorded on Saturday. But that's a giant leap. I definitely don't think he called her in. He'd have told the sheriff right away if that were the case."

"I agree with Briggs," King said. "Even if Austin had gone in, he'd have already said as much. I think that's just a dead end and we need to be looking at other possibilities."

Briggs just nodded.

"Who else might call her away?" Sadie asked. "Did she know anyone else here?"

"Not that I know of," Melissa said. "The only person I heard her talking to on the phone was her mom. And someone else that Kassie said was just a friend. Then she corrected herself and said he was more like a fan. I overheard her telling him not to come to Keating Hollow. Maybe he did and she's a victim of a crazed stalker."

Sadie sucked in a sharp breath. "That's scary. Did she say who the fan was?"

Melissa shook her head. "No. We didn't talk that much.

All I know is that she said her mother was a pretty awful stage mom, and she was certain that if she had the means, she'd be here to oversee the recording of the album."

King and Sadie shared a knowing look. Then King said, "Are you sure her mom didn't find a way here?"

"No, I'm not. Why?" Melissa asked.

"You know how crazy my mother was. It's possible that Kassie's mom is, too. Especially if she feels like Kassie isn't doing whatever she wants her to do."

"I know she wanted Kassie to send her money. Money Kassie doesn't have because she's already tapped out after covering her mom's bills," Melissa said. "You can't get blood from a stone, though, so I imagine she was pretty upset."

"Kassie also told me her mom was in debt to some pretty rough people," Briggs said. "Maybe they targeted Kassie in order to get at her mom."

"Someone should call her mother," King said, his eyes flashing with a darkness Melissa wasn't used to seeing. "Make sure she knows Kassie is missing and feel her out. Find out where she's at. If she did come to Keating Hollow, I'd put her as number one on the suspect list."

Melissa had heard that it was pretty common for crimes like this to be committed by close friends or even family members, and she thought King might be onto something. "I'll see if I can find a number to call her," Melissa said. "I'll touch base with her and let her know we're here for her during this crisis. See how she responds."

"We should also look into this Theo guy," Briggs said as he stared at his phone. "He's always commenting on Kassie's posts and talking about protecting her and keeping her safe from the ugly world. It's pretty creepy to be honest."

King walked over and peered over Briggs's shoulder as he looked at the social media page. "That guy lives just down the coast a few hours. Probably wouldn't be too hard to find him." He tapped his name into a search engine and in no time, he said, "Got him! His address is right there."

"Now what are you going to do with it?" Briggs asked him.

"Go have a chat." King looked at Sadie. "Want to come with me after we're done with lunch?"

"I'm sure as heck not letting you go by yourself," she said. "We know better than most how crazed fans can get."

King nodded. "You've got that right."

They quickly polished off the macaroni and cheese. After King put their bowls in the dishwasher, he said, "We're going to head down the coast. We'll be in touch." He met Melissa's gaze. "Let me know if you talk to her mom and how that goes."

"I will," she said and walked them to the door. After they left, she returned to the couch where Briggs had relocated and sat next to him.

He immediately wrapped his arm around her shoulders and pulled her in. "I missed you."

"I missed you, too," she said, resting her head on his shoulder. "I don't ever want to get another call like that again. I'm damned lucky I didn't get hauled in for reckless driving considering how fast I hightailed it back here after Sadie's call."

"I'm sorry. I hate that you were driving when she told

you what happened." Briggs pressed a soft kiss to her head. "I was worried about you, too."

She squeezed his hand. "I'm just glad we're here now." Melissa pushed herself up and went to find her own phone. Then she searched for Kassie's mother. It didn't take long to find her. She had her own website and contact number that was billed as management for her daughter. It was obvious that Norma Kinny would do what she had to in order to get a piece of Kassie's success.

The phone rang twice before a woman answered. "Norma Kinny, what'cha got?"

"Ms. Kinny?" Melissa asked.

"Isn't that what I just said?" the woman barked.

"I suppose it is," Melissa said. She introduced herself and then said, "I know this has to be a rough time for you since Kassie went missing yesterday morning, but I just wanted you to know that I'm here if you need anything."

"Kassie's not missing," the woman said, sounding disinterested. "The sheriff is over reacting. My daughter just does this sometimes. I wouldn't worry about it. She'll turn up."

"But, Ms. Kinny, didn't the sheriff tell you that there's video footage of her getting assaulted? And she didn't take any of her stuff," Melissa explained.

"Oh." There was a long pause. Then she said, "I'm a little strapped for cash right now. Can you send me funds so that I can get to Keating Hollow?"

"I'm sorry, you want me to send you money?" Melissa asked, taken aback.

"Yes. So I can get there and be there for my daughter.

You just said you're here for me if I need anything. You can Venmo me five hundred dollars. I'll text you my Venmo link."

"Five hundred?" Melissa parroted.

"Yes. For food and gas and lodging. You know what, it would be better if you sent six hundred."

The line went dead and then a text popped up for the woman's Venmo.

Melissa gaped at the phone. "She can't be serious."

Briggs took her phone, looked at the link, and shook his head. He tapped out a message and then handed the phone back.

It read, *Melissa is not your bank. Ask your husband for money.*

"She's married?" Melissa frowned at the phone. "Kassie didn't mention that."

"Yep. They are both grifters, but Kassie's stepdad has a job at the sanitation department. I'm pretty sure he just tells Kassie's mom he doesn't have any money because she'd spend it all."

"Then she guilts Kassie into covering her debts, is that it?" Melissa asked.

"You've got it."

Melissa felt sick as she thought about that scenario. She couldn't imagine having a mother who just used her for money. Melissa's mother usually wouldn't even let her buy lunch. Her mom always treated and called it her "mother's rights" to spoil her daughter.

Damn, she missed her mom. She'd have to make a point of calling her soon.

"Since Kassie's mom doesn't appear to be in town, I guess we can cross her off our list," Melissa said. "I feel like, unless King finds anything out, we've hit a dead end."

Briggs pressed his lips together and nodded. "I think the only thing left to do is ask Austin for the video footage outside the studio."

"Do you think he'd give it to you?"

"There's only one way to find out." Briggs tapped his screen and called his boss.

CHAPTER 23

*B*riggs had watched the video footage outside the recording studio so many times that his eyes were starting to blur.

"I just don't think there's anything we can glean from this," Melissa said, sounding just as frustrated as he felt.

"No. It's obvious that Kassie knows whoever she's talking to, but we never get a decent look at the guy," Briggs said. He didn't know why, but the way the guy moved scratched at his brain. It felt familiar, like he reminded Briggs of someone. But he just couldn't put his finger on it, and it was driving him insane.

"I think maybe we should just go to bed," Melissa said, rubbing her eyes. "It's been a long day."

He couldn't argue with her there.

King had called a few hours ago. The online harasser had actually been a seventeen-year-old kid who had a broken leg and had been laid up in bed for a few months.

When he'd learned that Kassie was missing, he'd started hyperventilating and wanted to know how he could help find her. Sadie had told him to leave it to the law enforcement investigators, and although he hadn't been happy with that, he'd finally relented. They were convinced he had nothing to do with Kassie's assault.

Since then, they'd been combing through clips from the studio, going over footage from the previous week to find out if there were any other suspicious meetings. There weren't. And Briggs had to agree with Melissa that they'd hit a dead end.

"Briggs?" Melissa asked. "Ready to hit the hay?"

"Yes." He stood and held her hand as they made their way to his bedroom. "You're sure you want to stay over?"

She just scoffed at him. "You can try to get rid of me, but it won't work."

Briggs chuckled softly. "Not me. All I want to do is get you naked and forget the last couple of days ever happened."

"I'm in."

He met her gaze and then swept her up in his arms and took her to bed.

Briggs woke just as the birds started to chirp and the sun started to rise. He looked over at Melissa, who was buried under the covers and sleeping peacefully. He was glad someone had slept. He'd only gotten a few hours before he'd woken, his mind racing with what could have happened to Kassie. He hated that they didn't have any leads. Hated it even more that he hadn't asked her more about her life so that he'd have a clue of where to start.

After carefully rolling out of bed, Briggs pulled on sweats and a T-shirt and padded into his kitchen. While he waited for his coffee to brew, he scrolled through Kassie's social media again, searching for something—anything—that might give them a place to start looking.

He found nothing other than her clickbait posts. They weren't all about Briggs and King. Some were about her label, and some were about entitled fans. One even called out a restaurant that refused to substitute a salad for french fries. But none of them were too over the top. Nothing that would trigger someone to drive hours to Keating Hollow to abduct her.

The first hit of caffeine was a welcome reprieve, helping to clear the cobwebs from his mind. He quickly grabbed a bagel with a smear of cream cheese and then sat at his table, staring at Kassie's social media picture. She was holding her phone and making a face as if she'd just read a text she wasn't thrilled about.

It reminded him of all the texts she'd sent him while she'd been on the road. All the messages he hadn't read. He opened up the text chain and started to scan her ramblings.

There was a lot of small talk about her tour, and sexy talk about what she wanted to do with him once she got back in town, and a lot of swearing when he didn't text her back. But then he hit on a string of messages that were all about her mom and stepdad.

That's when things got interesting.

Her stepdad had actually followed her around for a few

shows. He'd been there, demanding money to pay her mother's debts. And then finally one where she implied that he'd threatened her.

He reread the text again.

Wayne was just here. He's angry. Said he didn't want to have to be here, but my mother gave him no choice. That if I didn't give him the money to pay for her facelift that I'd regret it. In the end, I just gave him the money. It was worth it to get rid of him.

Briggs snuck back into his room, quietly got dressed, and then left Melissa a note. It was still early, and he didn't want to wake her, but he needed to talk to Sheriff Baker ASAP.

With his phone tucked into his pocket, he hurried out to his truck.

But when he pushed the button to start it, nothing happened. "What the hell?" he muttered.

"Get out of the truck," a man ordered from outside of the vehicle.

Briggs looked over and froze when he saw a gun was pointed at his head.

"Out. Now." The man, who appeared to be in his late forties or early fifties, had a receding hairline and a crooked nose. He didn't look to be messing around.

"All right. I'm getting out," Briggs said.

The man took two steps back and waited.

Very slowly, Briggs reached for the door handle and pushed the door open. Once he had his feet on the ground, he raised his hands in the air. "What do you want?"

"You know my daughter, Kassie?"

Daughter? Was this her stepdad? It had to be. Kassie had

told him her biological father had passed away when she was very young. "I know Kassie."

"You're the one she's been living with?" he asked.

"She had been staying at my house, yes," Briggs said.

"Good. Let's go inside. She has something of mine." He waved his gun, indicating that Briggs should move.

"She moved out a week ago," Briggs said, his heart racing. The last thing he was going to do was let this man in his house where Melissa was sleeping. "She has been staying with a friend of mine."

The man's nostrils flared. "If you're lying to me, I'll put a bullet in your chest."

Briggs's magic tingled at the base of his spine, but he couldn't risk losing control. He didn't know what would happen. If the gun went off, he didn't want to be on the smoking end of it. He also couldn't risk doing any damage to the man until he found out if he was holding Kassie captive. "I'm not lying. I can take you there if you want."

"Move it." The man swung his weapon again, making Briggs want to duck, but he did his best to keep his cool. "Go out onto the road to the silver Honda."

Briggs did as he was told and prayed it wasn't too late to find Kassie.

CHAPTER 24

Melissa woke with a start. Her heart was racing, and a headache had formed just above her right eye. She glanced around at the empty bedroom. "Briggs?"

Silence.

She sat on the edge of the bed, trying to calm her nerves, and then rose and wrapped herself in Briggs's robe that was hanging on the back of his bathroom door.

The house was silent as she made her way to the kitchen, making her wonder where in the hell Briggs had gone. She peeked out the front window and spotted his truck. That meant he had to be there somewhere, right?

After making herself a cup of coffee, she wandered the house, looking for any sign of him.

Nothing.

It was like he'd just vanished.

But then she saw the note.

Mel, I've gone to talk to Sheriff Baker. I'll be back soon.

What did he have to say to the sheriff? She went back into the bedroom, found her phone, and called Briggs. When it went straight to voice mail, she frowned.

Something was off. She could feel it in her bones. It was as if she could feel Briggs's anxiety reaching out to her. Was the sheriff giving him a hard time? What exactly had he wanted to talk to him about? The questions were driving her crazy as she paced his living room.

Then when the sun glinted off the chrome of Briggs's truck, she stopped in her tracks. His truck was parked right outside. Unless someone had come to pick him up, he hadn't gone anywhere.

She called Sadie.

"Morning. Everything okay?"

"No," Melissa said. "Did King come get Briggs this morning?"

"No. He's right here. Why? Was he supposed to?"

"I don't know. I found a note that Briggs left, telling me that he went to the sheriff's department, but his truck is here and he's not answering his phone. Do you think they arrested him again?" Melissa sucked in a sharp breath. "I gotta go. I need to call them and find out what's happening."

"Call me when you know something," Sadie said just before Melissa ended the call.

Melissa dialed the sheriff's office and was told that no one had been sent to pick up Briggs, nor had they seen him that morning.

"But he's not here, and he said he was going there," Melissa said, though she wasn't expecting an answer.

"If I see him, I'll tell him you're looking for him," Clarissa, the receptionist, said.

"Thanks." Melissa ended the call, sank into the chair by the front door, and closed her eyes. She focused on that anxious feeling, the one that just felt like it was coming from Briggs. And in her mind, she screamed, *Where are you?*

Immediately, a vision of her own house flashed in her mind.

My house? she thought. Why would he be there?

The feeling intensified. She didn't question it. She just knew that she had to move. After throwing on some clothes, she ran outside to Briggs's truck. But when she pushed the button, it didn't do anything. The engine didn't even turn over.

She let out a frustrated cry and called Sadie again.

"What did you find out?" Sadie asked.

"I think Briggs is at my house. Can you go check on him?"

"Check on him, why?" she asked.

"Something's wrong."

"Oh. Oh no. I would, Melissa, but we're not home. We're just out of town at the eastern trailhead. King and I took a morning hike."

"Are you on your way back? Can you pick me up? I'm stranded and… Just, please, Sadie."

There must have been more panic in Melissa's tone than she realized, because Sadie didn't hesitate. She just said, "We're on our way."

Melissa was waiting outside when King's Toyota turned

into the driveway. She ran and jumped into the backseat. "Go!"

The entire way into town, the tingle of anxiety grew. Briggs was barely hanging on, and she just knew if she didn't get there soon, something terrible was going to happen.

"Faster," she ordered.

King just nodded and sped up. A few minutes later, he slammed to a stop in her driveway.

Melissa didn't wait. She jumped out of the vehicle and ran inside the house.

The moment her door slammed open, she heard a loud crash followed by a loud roar of frustration.

"Briggs!" She bolted down her hallway toward the noise and came to a dead stop when she spotted a man pinning Briggs to the floor. He had a gun pointed at Briggs's chest and was shaking with rage.

Melissa felt the slippery ropes of magic cling to her mind, and without any thought at all, she sent it straight toward the man. In her mind's eye, the magic coiled around him.

He froze and looked around the room. When his gaze landed on Melissa he said, "Let me go, or your boyfriend will need a pine box."

She didn't bother to answer him. Instead, she envisioned the gun flying out of his hand and watched as it sailed into the closet and fell harmlessly into a pile of Kassie's clothes.

The man opened his mouth to rage at her, but the magical bindings tightened further, and they were so suffocating he couldn't get the words out.

Briggs pushed the man off himself and sat up. "Call the sheriff. Kassie is in trouble!"

Melissa dialed 911 and then handed the phone to Briggs.

"The man who abducted Kassie Kinny has been apprehended. Send someone over right away. And send someone to the Emerald Caves before the tide comes in. You'll find Kassie there."

"The Emerald Caves?" Melissa asked with a gasp as she kneeled beside him. "He left her there?"

Briggs nodded, looking exhausted as he thanked the dispatcher on the other end of the line. When he ended it, he looked at Melissa. "He left her there as an insurance policy to get what he wanted. If we didn't cooperate, he'd let her drown."

"What did he want?" Melissa asked.

Briggs held up a safe-deposit box key. "This. It holds valuable jewels left to her by her paternal grandparents. He wanted them so he could pawn them. Or sell them at auction maybe. He seems to think they are worth a pretty penny."

King walked into the room with Deputy Hunt on his heels. Hunt went straight for Kassie's stepfather and tried to cuff him, but he couldn't get past Melissa's magical bindings. He looked at Melissa and asked, "Do you mind?"

"Oh, sorry," she said sheepishly. "I'm not used to wielding magic."

Briggs grinned at her, and she grinned back.

"Could have fooled me," the deputy muttered as he slapped the cuffs on the man and then yanked him to his feet.

"His weapon is in the closet," Melissa said.

"Forensics will be in here shortly to search for evidence," he said and then frog-marched the man out of Melissa's house.

"What happened?" Melissa asked Briggs as they sat there waiting for the police to do whatever they needed to do.

Briggs sucked in a deep breath and then let it out. It was as if all the tension he carried just melted away. Melissa felt it, too. That anxiety that had been eating away at her had suddenly eased, and her headache was gone.

"I was looking through my phone and found an old message from Kassie that raised some red flags about her stepdad, so I was going to head to the station to show them to the sheriff. But that jackass intercepted me. I thought he wanted money, but it turned out, he was looking for that safe-deposit box key. He made me search this room until I found it."

"While holding you at gunpoint, right?" Melissa said, her ire rising.

"Yeah. And then when I found it, I wouldn't give it to him until he told me where Kassie was. Since he didn't really care about her at all, he told me right away. When he heard you burst in, he tackled me for it. But then you came in like a superhero queen, saved me, and captured him. If there's any justice, he'll be in jail for a long time."

"One can only hope," Melissa said.

It took about an hour for the investigators to go through everything in Kassie's room and interview both Briggs and Melissa. When they were finally about to leave, Sheriff

RISE OF THE WITCH

Baker called one of his deputies and told them to put Briggs on the phone.

"Yes, Sheriff?" Briggs said. He listened for a couple minutes, thanked the sheriff, and then handed the phone back to the officer.

"What did he want?" King asked.

"Kassie is safe. They got to her just in time, and they are now taking her to Healer Whipple to be looked at." Briggs squeezed Melissa's hand. "She's safe because of you."

"And you," Melissa assured him. "You're the one who pried the information out of her stepdad."

Briggs nodded and then got to his feet. He held his hand out to Melissa. "Ready?"

"Where are we going?" she asked, already falling in step beside him.

"To Healer Whipple's office to see Kassie."

Melissa's heart swelled with emotion for how kind her boyfriend was. She knew that Kassie wasn't his favorite person, but he was thoughtful enough to make sure someone familiar was there for her after her traumatic abduction.

Melissa let King and Sadie know they could go as Briggs walked out to her car. She held Briggs's hand the entire time she drove them to the healer's office. She just felt the need to be touching him. He seemed to be on the same wavelength, because once they parked and were headed into the clinic, he wrapped his arm around her and kept her close. It was exactly what they both needed.

As soon as they walked into the clinic and told the receptionist that they were there to see Kassie, they were quickly ushered down the hall and into her room. She sat at the end of the exam table, wrapped in a thick wool blanket. She took one look at them and asked, "Did you castrate that bastard?"

Melissa couldn't help it. She laughed. "No, but I wish I could have."

"Me, too," she said with a sneer. "Maybe someone in prison will take care of that for us." Then she held her arms out and said, "Both of you come here and give me a hug."

They did as she asked, and as she held on tight, she whispered, "Thank you."

When they finally pulled away, she wiped the tears from her eyes and said, "Now, someone get Healer Whipple to discharge me. I'm ready to go home."

Melissa squeezed her hand. "I'm ready for you to go home, too."

"Do you mean my home in LA, or…" Kassie asked, looking worried.

"No, not LA," Melissa said with a soft chuckle. "The one here, with me, in Keating Hollow."

Kassie wiped at her eyes again as her lips curved up into a hint of a smile.

CHAPTER 25

Briggs sat at his dining room table and listened to Melissa chatter on about how she was actually enjoying living with Kassie now, and he smiled into his cup. He knew that within a few minutes, Kassie would text with some issue or question or demand, and Melissa would be silently cursing her again.

Despite the minor irritations, they really did seem to be getting along now that Kassie's stepfather was in jail and her mother had stopped talking to her. She blamed Kassie for her husband going to jail. It seemed she'd blocked out the part about him kidnapping Kassie and holding Briggs at gunpoint.

It didn't matter though. Kassie was glad for the silence. She was getting her finances in order and had toned down the clickbait posts on social media. That didn't mean she didn't post questionable things anymore, but at least she was reasonable about taking them down if someone objected.

"She even unloaded the dishwasher, Briggs. I'm telling you, it's progress," Melissa said as she bustled around the kitchen, making breakfast. They'd started taking turns making breakfast for each other, and it was her morning.

Briggs eyed the waffles on the plate she was still holding. "Do I get to eat those, or are you saving them for your other boyfriend?"

She glanced down at them and chuckled as she handed them over. "Sorry. Guess I got a little distracted."

He brushed a kiss over her cheek and said, "Thank you. They smell delicious."

Melissa beamed at him, and he thought he'd never get tired of seeing her pretty face in the mornings.

Life had been pretty good lately. All the charges against Briggs had been dropped, and the sheriff had issued him a formal apology. He'd also gotten answers as to why he'd been the one implicated in the abduction.

Kassie had admitted to picking up his credit card the night they'd had dinner. She'd said she wasn't really going to use it, but Briggs had his doubts. When someone was struggling financially, they did some pretty shady things. He'd seen it far too often while living in foster care. The morning that her stepfather attacked and abducted her, she'd offered it as a bargaining chip for him to let her go. But he wasn't interested. All he wanted was that safe-deposit box key.

As for the flannel, it turned out that Wayne had actually

stolen it out of Briggs's truck the night before when he'd been watching Briggs and Kassie. He'd participated in enough criminal activity over the years that he'd picked up a few tricks. One of them was making sure you dressed in someone else's clothes so that you weren't implicated when the law came knocking.

Kassie had finally accessed the safe-deposit box after months of avoiding it so that her mom and stepdad couldn't get their hands on any of it, and then she sold a couple pieces at auction to get herself out of debt.

King hadn't told her, but he'd purchased both pieces just in case she wanted them back some day. Their song had released a few days ago and had immediately climbed to #1 on the charts. It was still there, with King and Sadie's song at #2.

All the success had brought the paparazzi back to town. There had only been a few articles accusing King and Briggs of being a couple. Kassie had even gone on record to retract her earlier comments about them being boyfriends.

The rising pop star hadn't changed *all* her spots yet, but she was working on it. And since she was still living with Melissa—and paying rent—they'd all made an effort to include her. She and Melissa and Sadie were all friends, and it was the happiest Briggs had ever seen her.

"What do you think I should bring to cards tonight?" Melissa asked him.

He turned his attention to her and frowned. "You have to bring something to cards? Like what? Some sort of game?"

"No, no. Imogen is handling that. Sadie and I are supposed to bring desserts. I need to make something, and I'm not sure which direction to go."

"Oh, I see." The doorbell rang, and as Briggs got up to get the door, he called, "Snickerdoodles!"

"I knew you'd say that," she called back.

"Then why'd you ask me?" He chuckled and opened the door to find a tall man about his age with thick black hair standing on his porch. "Can I help you?"

The man peered at him and then visibly swallowed. There was something eerily familiar about him, but Briggs wasn't sure why.

"Brandon?" the man asked, wonder and relief shining in his eyes. "Is that you?"

Briggs felt a rush of warmth running through his veins, followed quickly by that anxious dread he got when he was reminded of his childhood. "Dutton?"

"Oh my gods, it is you," Dutton said as his eyes misted with emotion. "I can't believe I finally found you."

"Who's this?" Melissa said as she strolled up behind Briggs.

"I'm Brandon's brother, Dutton." He held out his hand. "And you are?"

Briggs felt Melissa tense beside him and quickly squeezed her hand. "It's okay, Mel. He's my older brother from my biological parents. I just haven't seen him since…"

"It's been over fifteen years," Dutton said. "Not since the night we were both put into foster care."

Briggs's heart was beating loudly in his own ears. Had he

heard him correctly? Dutton had been forced into foster care, too?

"I can see you two have a lot to catch up on," Melissa said carefully. "Briggs? Are you going to invite your brother in?"

"Huh? Oh, right. Of course. This way." He held the door open for him and gestured for him to take a seat on the couch. "Do you need anything? Water? Coffee? A shot of whiskey?"

Dutton chuckled. "Maybe just water."

"I'll get it," Melissa said. "I'll be right back."

The two brothers sat down across from each other. Neither said anything as they took in the other one. Dutton was a slightly taller version of Briggs, only he had bright blue eyes and a dimple in his left cheek. Briggs guessed he'd never had trouble catching the eye of the opposite sex. Not that he'd ever had to worry about that either.

Finally, Briggs's curiosity got the best of him. "What are you doing here, Dutton?"

"I came to find you," he said simply.

"Okay, but why now?"

Dutton pressed his lips together as he leaned forward and rested his elbows on his knees. "I've been looking for you since I was twenty years old, Brandon."

"It's Briggs now," he corrected.

"Right. Briggs. Sorry." Dutton gave his brother a small smile. "I read that, but seeing you in person, I just see my little brother again, and that makes my brain short-circuit a little."

"I won't lie. Mine's not exactly firing on all cylinders at the moment either," Briggs confessed. "It's kind of blowing my mind seeing you here." He hadn't ever really expected to see his brother or his parents again. He and his brother hadn't exactly been close growing up, but that was likely because their father always pitted them against each other.

"I read about that singer being abducted in an article the other day. Kassie Kinny? And somewhere in the article they mentioned you by your given name. I wasn't sure it would be you. Williams is such a common last name that I was afraid to get my hopes up, but when I saw your picture and then found you online via Kassie Kinny's and King McGrath's social media pages, I knew it was you. And here I am."

But why? Briggs wanted to ask. What was the real reason? "Okay, you found me. Now what?" he asked with a smile.

Dutton glanced at the floor and then back up at him. "I just want my family back, Bran—Briggs. And you're the only family I've ever had. That's all."

Briggs swallowed hard. He knew what it was like to have no one. He'd been there before King had come along. He recognized the haunted look in Dutton's eyes and nodded. "Okay. How long are you in town?"

He shrugged. "Not sure."

"Do you have a place to stay?"

"I was going to try the inn if it turned out that you're really my brother," he said as he got to his feet. "I should go see if they have a vacancy."

Briggs scrambled to get up and put his hand out to stop him. "You don't need a room at the inn. You can stay here."

Dutton stared at him, his eyes searching his brother's face. Then he said, "Are you sure?"

"I'm positive. Go get your stuff. We'll get you set up in the guest room."

His brother gave him a slow, easy smile and then nodded. "I think I'd like that."

As Dutton went outside to get his luggage, Melissa came up behind Briggs and wrapped her arms around him. "Are you sure this is a good idea?"

He laughed softly. "No, but the offer's been made. I guess we're about to find out."

She kissed the side of his neck. "You know what? It's never a bad thing to have more people to love."

He leaned back against her, enjoying her soft touch and the warmth she radiated from within, and nodded. Then he chuckled and said, "I'm pretty sure he owes me a wrestling match. Better watch out. The last time we wrestled, we nearly broke the television."

She just shrugged. "It's your furniture. What you do to it is your business."

"It is now, but someday it's gonna be yours, too."

"Is it?" she asked with a raised eyebrow.

"Definitely. Because make no mistake, Melissa Benson. I fully intend to marry you one day. One day soon."

"That's good," she shot back. "Because I already picked out a dress."

He waited for the panic to settle in, and when it didn't, he spun her around and kissed her until she was breathless.

"Should I reconsider that room at the inn?" Dutton asked.

They both laughed.

"No," Briggs said as he winked at Melissa. "Let me show you to the guest room."

And as he helped Dutton get settled in, Briggs felt a contentment he'd never known before and grinned when his brother turned to him and asked, "Ready for that wrestling match?"

CHAPTER 26

VALENTINE'S DAY

*D*utton Williams followed his brother Briggs and Brigg's girlfriend Melissa into the barn at Imogen Thane's property. The tables were in the shape of hearts with red bouquets of flowers for centerpieces. Soft candlelight illuminated the space, giving it the expected romantic feel. He had to admit that the space was elegant and inviting… if one were there with a date or significant other.

For a solo like him, it was just depressing.

He was kicking himself for letting Briggs and Melissa talk him into going to this party that Imogen had arranged. They'd promised live music, dancing, and good food. Along with other singles in Keating Hollow who were looking to do something other than spend the night alone.

Maybe that would all be true eventually as the night wore on. But at the moment, it looked like everyone was paired up, and the only thing to drink was champagne.

Dutton did not drink booze with bubbles in it.

Melissa glanced over at him and grimaced slightly. "Sorry. I was told this would be a party and wasn't just for Valentines."

"Don't worry about it," he said. "I should have known."

Dutton had been in Keating Hollow for a little over three weeks now. He'd come after a particularly painful breakup. Though he hadn't told anyone that. He'd just wanted to settle in and get to know his brother again. After years of being separated, he was really enjoying his time with Briggs. It turned out that they got along really well and in just a short time, Dutton had already decided to make Keating Hollow his permanent residence.

Just as soon as he found a place of his own. Which wasn't proving to be easy. But his brother didn't seem to mind him staying in his guest room, and for that he was grateful.

Because going back to San Diego was out of the question.

The mess he'd left back there… He didn't need to revisit that any time soon. Or ever as far as he was concerned.

Walking in on his bride and her supposed best friend while they were going at it in Dutton's bed the morning of his wedding had really done a number on him.

Now all he wanted was to spend some time hiking in the mountains, find a place to live, and open a classic car restoration shop. Since he'd just sold his house in San Diego, all of those things were feasible. He just needed to make it happen.

Someday soon. Probably.

Once he didn't feel like he'd just had the crap kicked out of him.

He glanced around at all the happy couples and decided he definitely needed something stronger than champagne.

"I'll be right back," he told Briggs and Melissa, who were already half a glass into the bubbly. "I've got to find something stronger than this."

"Good luck, man," Briggs said. "If you find whiskey, let me know."

Dutton nodded and left the couples' party. The barn wasn't the only place holding an event that night.

Off in the right side of the field, there was a tent set up and guests were already starting to arrive at the wedding being held next door.

A horseless carriage pulled up and parked at the edge of the parking area, no doubt waiting for the bride and groom to come running out after saying their vows.

That just wasn't anything he needed to see. Not in his state of mind. He turned his back on the scene and worked his way over to a food truck area that was set up around an ice-skating rink.

Jackpot.

Not only was there a cash bar, but there was a dessert truck, too. He first ordered a piece of carrot cake and once he had that in hand, he ordered a whiskey and soda and went off to find a place to enjoy his guilty pleasures in peace.

It didn't take him long to find a bench that was positioned under a large oak tree. He took a seat and watched as couple after couple arrived to celebrate the holiday.

He finished off his cake and then downed his drink far faster than he intended. It just meant he needed another drink. When he got to the cash bar, he frowned when he spotted a gorgeous woman in her formfitting wedding dress standing at the cart, ordering a vodka and tonic.

"Better make it two," she said with a hitch in her voice.

Dutton stood behind her, giving her space, but when she turned around, she startled and spilled an entire drink right down the front of her dress.

"Damn," she said, shaking her head.

"I am so sorry," he said, completely mortified. "I didn't mean to scare you. I was actually trying to give you space."

"Space. That's what I need," she said with a nod. "Plenty of space. Like a Grand Canyon-sized space." She opened her arms wide and spilled the second drink. "Because no bride wants to hear on the day of her wedding that her groom isn't sure he wants to get married. Like, that's the worst thing that could happen, right?"

"Maybe not the worst," Dutton said. "He could have run off with the best man or maid of honor."

She let out a bark of laughter. "That I could understand. You know? But just not being sure, like he somehow entered into this commitment without a thought in the world? Who does that?"

Dutton didn't feel qualified for this conversation, but he tried anyway. "Maybe he just has a bad case of nerves?"

"Maybe he's just a jackass." She ordered another drink and then walked off toward the wedding venue.

"Thank the gods that's not me," he muttered, remembering all too well what it was like to be dressed and ready to say I do only to turn around and tell everyone the ceremony was canceled due to the bride being unable to control herself around other men. It had been a petty thing to say, but he just didn't give a damn in the moment.

Dutton got two more whiskey and sodas, one for him and one for his brother, and then started to make his way back to the sock hop, where the lovebirds were probably declaring their love to each other every three minutes when doves were released into the air. Or some crap like that.

He'd just about made it to the barn when he heard hushed arguing.

"I will not marry you," the woman in the wedding dress said. "Not after you told me you needed space."

"I just said I was having doubts," the groom argued. "That I needed to talk to Blossom to make sure I wasn't making a mistake."

"Blossom is your ex-girlfriend, you jackass!" She threw her drink in his face and started to run toward the parking area.

"Dahlia, wait!" The groom took off and easily caught up with the bride.

Dutton was going to leave them to their fight and let them work it out, but when he saw the groom grab the bride and shake her as if he were trying to shake some sense into her, he couldn't leave it alone. He strode over and pulled the man off her.

There were tears in her eyes as she backed away from the groom.

"Are you all right?" he asked her.

She nodded, but her eyes were wide with shock.

"This doesn't have anything to do with you," the groom sneered. "Why don't you mind your own business?"

"I was going to until I saw you hurting this woman. Now it's too late to act like I didn't see anything," Dutton said.

"I did no such thing," the groom insisted and then reached for her again.

When she flinched, Dutton sprang into action, sweeping the bride up off her feet and striding away from the abusive jackass.

"Where to?" he asked her.

She swallowed hard and said, "Anywhere. Just get me out of here."

He would have been happy to drive her anywhere she wanted to go, but he didn't have a vehicle. "Do you have a car here?"

She shook her head. "My sister drove me."

"Right. The carriage it is then." He jogged over to the horseless carriage, helped her get in, and then climbed in after her. Out of thin air, a voice asked, "Where to, sir and madam?"

"Anywhere, Jeeves," Dutton ordered. "Just floor it. We have a runaway bride."

DEANNA'S BOOK LIST

Witches of Keating Hollow:
Soul of the Witch
Heart of the Witch
Spirit of the Witch
Dreams of the Witch
Courage of the Witch
Love of the Witch
Power of the Witch
Essence of the Witch
Muse of the Witch
Vision of the Witch
Waking of the Witch
Honor of the Witch
Promise of the Witch
Return of the Witch
Fortune of the Witch
Song of the Witch

Rise of the Witch
Charm of the Witch

Keating Hollow Happily Ever Afters:
Gift of the Witch
Wisdom of the Witch
Light of the Witch
Spell of the Witch

Witches of Befana Bay:
The Witch's Silver Lining
The Witch's Secret Love
The Witch's Lost Spell
The Witch's Hidden Garden

Witches of Christmas Grove:
A Witch For Mr. Holiday
A Witch For Mr. Christmas
A Witch For Mr. Winter
A Witch For Mr. Mistletoe
A Witch For Mr. Frost
A Witch For Mr. Garland
A Witch For Mr. Bell

Premonition Pointe Novels:
Witching For Grace
Witching For Hope
Witching For Joy
Witching For Clarity
Witching For Moxie

Witching For Kismet

Miss Matched Midlife Dating Agency:
Star-crossed Witch
Honor-bound Witch
Outmatched Witch
Moonstruck Witch
Rainmaker Witch

Jade Calhoun Novels:
Haunted on Bourbon Street
Witches of Bourbon Street
Demons of Bourbon Street
Angels of Bourbon Street
Shadows of Bourbon Street
Incubus of Bourbon Street
Bewitched on Bourbon Street
Hexed on Bourbon Street
Dragons of Bourbon Street

Pyper Rayne Novels:
Spirits, Stilettos, and a Silver Bustier
Spirits, Rock Stars, and a Midnight Chocolate Bar
Spirits, Beignets, and a Bayou Biker Gang
Spirits, Diamonds, and a Drive-thru Daiquiri Stand
Spirits, Spells, and Wedding Bells

Ida May Chronicles:
Witched To Death
Witch, Please

DEANNA'S BOOK LIST

Stop Your Witchin'

Crescent City Fae Novels:
Influential Magic
Irresistible Magic
Intoxicating Magic

Last Witch Standing:
Bewitched by Moonlight
Soulless at Sunset
Bloodlust By Midnight
Bitten At Daybreak

Witch Island Brides:
The Wolf's New Year Bride
The Vampire's Last Dance
The Warlock's Enchanted Kiss
The Shifter's First Bite

Destiny Novels:
Defining Destiny
Accepting Fate

Wolves of the Rising Sun:
Jace
Aiden
Luc
Craved
Silas
Darien

Wren

Black Bear Outlaws:
Cyrus
Chase
Cole

Bayou Springs Alien Mail Order Brides:
Zeke
Gunn
Echo

ABOUT THE AUTHOR

New York Times and USA Today bestselling author, Deanna Chase, is a native Californian, transplanted to the slower paced lifestyle of southeastern Louisiana and the Pacific Northwest. When she isn't writing, she is often goofing off with her husband, traveling, or playing with her two dogs. For more information and updates on newest releases visit her website at deannachase.com.

Made in United States
North Haven, CT
14 September 2025